Down Came a Blackbird

Also by Nicholas Wilde
Into the Dark
Death Knell

Down Came a Blackbird

Nicholas Wilde

Henry Holt and Company ◆ New York

First American edition
Published by Henry Holt and Company, Inc.,
115 West 18th Street, New York, New York 10011.
Originally published in Great Britain by HarperCollins of London.

Library of Congress Cataloging-in-Publication Data
Wilde, Nicholas.
Down came a blackbird / Nicholas Wilde.
"Originally published in Great Britain by HarperCollins of London"—T.p. verso.
Summary: Thirteen-year-old James, a social case with a criminal
record, withdraws into himself when sent to his great-uncle's estate
while his alcoholic mother is in the hospital, but strange dreams of
a boy who once lived on the estate help him rediscover his emotions.
ISBN 0-8050-2001-2
[1. Space and time—Fiction.   2. Uncles—Fiction.
3. Emotional problems—Fiction.]   I. Title.
PZ7.W64582Do   1991 [Fic]—dc20   92-20209

Printed in the United States of America
on acid-free paper. ∞
1 3 5 7 9 10 8 6 4 2

To Paul

1

The blackbird stopped its singing. It cocked its head, alert. There was danger.

From its bough, it looked down at the garden. An old garden, this part never used now. Willow herb, nettles, convolvulus, ivy. A sea of long grasses away to the copse and the lake. It had reverted, back to the wild, to a time when the house hadn't been here. But now, since this morning, something was different. A new track had opened, a pathway of beaten-down stems.

The blackbird listened, probing the stillness. No noise, and no movement. But there was danger all the same. A hidden presence somewhere, waiting poised.

A sound now, faintly, from the far side of the house where the lawns were, and the roses. Voices, the man and woman talking. But they had always been there. The menace didn't come from them.

The voices faded. The sense of threat, of being watched in secret, came again. The bird watched back, only its eye moving. Its body had coiled rigid, like a spring.

Then suddenly it saw him. Crouched low, down among the bushes, wrist cocked, fingers tensed on something that was glinting. His eyes took aim, unblinking, and the bird felt their resentment. Resentment against everything that lived and sang.

The boy's wrist moved. The steel spike flashed upward. With a sudden scream of warning, the blackbird sped to safety. It heard the thud behind it, metal into wood.

2

James's lip tightened on his teeth.

"Sod it," he said.

He listened to the cretinous squawking as the bird went bolting off into the copse. Then he thrust his way clear of the bushes and looked up at the oak tree. He'd missed by less than an inch. The dart was embedded in the bough.

"I'll get it next time. Kebab it."

A pity it hadn't been this time. It would've helped. If anything *could* help at the moment, that is, which he doubted. Rock bottom. And he'd probably even lost his dart.

He looked up at it again, then scanned the tree critically. It might be OK. The dart was only about halfway along one of the larger boughs and the tree was crabby enough to offer plenty of footholds. He'd tackled worse than this in his time. He decided it was climbable.

"A bit of luck for once."

The first bit of luck in thirteen years. God must be losing his touch.

He stepped across and took a grip on the bark, then he paused. Unless the bough was rotten, of course, which he'd probably find out when he was halfway along it. He measured the distance with his eye: a twelve-foot drop into old bricks and nettles. Well, so what. They'd be sorry then that they'd made him come here, to people he didn't know and didn't want to.

He glanced in the direction of the house. On the far side, where the window was open, the voices of his great-uncle and the housekeeper-woman had stopped now, so they must have cleared off to some other room out of earshot. He was glad. He hadn't liked what he'd seen of either of them in the hour since he'd got here. But he presumably wasn't meant to. All part of the punishment for what he'd done, he supposed.

He hoisted himself up through a skein of ivy to the lower branches. Twigs fractured, dry and dead as dust. Then he clambered his way on round the trunk, trying not to look down at what he'd land in if the bough did the same as the twigs.

It'd serve them right when they noticed he was missing and came and found him down there. If they noticed. They probably wouldn't. Maybe he'd end up on two sticks, like this great-uncle he'd been brought here to live with. He wondered if the old bloke had smashed up his legs climbing trees. It was unlikely by the look of him, he wasn't the tree-climbing sort. The war probably . . . There might be another war some day. James fervently hoped there would be, before he was too old for it. He'd show them then, he'd wipe out the lot of them.

The lower branches thinned and his head emerged above them, giving him his first clear view of the lie of the land.

Beyond the tangle of hedge which closed off this section of garden he could see the house front, longways-on, with the open window at the end farthest from him. Shrubs and rose beds, lawns like a park, and the long gravel driveway he'd been driven up when he'd arrived here.

He leaned farther out, to his left.

He could see the stone steps now, up to the door where he'd stood with his Puma bag, waiting. And the brass bell-pull the probation bloke had made some feeble joke about because he'd been even more nervous than James was. It was the housekeeper-woman who'd opened the door. She'd smiled at him, twisting her hands in a cloth, and made some feeble joke, too. Then she'd looked at his bag and her smiling had stopped, as if she couldn't believe that one little bag was all that he'd got. Well, it *was* all he'd got, so she'd just have to lump it.

He'd been glad to get out of there. They hadn't needed him anyway. The probation bloke had probably filled them in on all the personal details. But at least he'd gone now: the car had driven off about quarter of an hour ago. So that was that. He was stuck here.

He turned his head, away from the neat stretch of lawns to the part of the garden he'd come to. So different from the rest that it was hard to believe it belonged to the house at all. By the look of it, no one had touched it for years.

"God-forsaken dump."

On second thought, though, God probably *hadn't* forsaken it. He was more likely to be hanging around down there somewhere, to have a good laugh at his next dirty trick. The breaking-bough trick. Well, he'd better make the most of it; it'd be the last laugh he'd get out of James Edward Greville. Those bricks would crack open skulls like eggshells.

James heaved himself out. The bough didn't break. He straddled his way along it on palms and buttocks, out into space. This was the feeling he liked best. It was what made him still want to climb trees. He was untouchable up here.

He prized the dart free and clamped it lengthwise between his teeth, then almost regretfully he made his way back to the trunk. He stayed there a while in the cleft, smoothing the red flight feathers and polishing the spike on his jeans as he gazed out at the house. He wasn't going to go back there yet. They'd probably be glad if he didn't show up at all. It wasn't the sort of place that fancied thirteen-year-old social cases with one Puma bag.

Great barn of a thing. Georgian, the probation bloke had said, a Georgian country house. The sort of place they used in old films. Much bigger than he'd been used to, or expected. But weird-looking, not big *enough*, somehow. He frowned. The shape was all wrong. It was as if it hadn't been finished on this side or something, as if it just stopped dead when it reached this disused bit of the garden. Maybe worth investigating later . . . He studied the end wall facing him. Three or four floors high, and thick with old ivy right up to the eaves. So where were the windows?

"Creepy."

Then he froze. A voice had come.

"James!"

She was there, the housekeeper-woman, on the front step. From the height of his bough he could see her, really small. She'd come out of the house and was looking. He pressed himself hard to the trunk.

"James?"

Why couldn't she just leave him alone? Why couldn't they all just get off his back?

"Teatime, James."

She looked round again, and went in.

James clenched the dart in his fist and stabbed it in and out of the bough. Teatime. Bloo-dy-tea-time. Tea-bloo-dy-time. There were going to be *times* here, then. Right times for doing things, wrong times for doing things. Lunchtime, teatime, suppertime. Time to go for a wash, James. Time to go to bed, James. She was going to be the same as all the rest. Teachers, social workers, psychiatrists. *Just give*

it time, James.—Time's on your side, James.—Time you re-
formed, James.—Go on like this, James, and you'll end up doing
time.

"Sod the lot of them!"

He stabbed again, hilt-deep. He wrenched the dart free
and pressed the point on his hand till it hurt. Then he turned
his head. Another sound had come. From the distant copse,
it rippled towards him. It was the blackbird's song. His face
tightened with pain.

He looked down at the dart which was gripped in his
fingers, and watched the bead of crimson as it flowered in
his palm.

3

"Oh there you are, James."

The housekeeper-woman smiled at him and hesitated, as if she was expecting an answer. She didn't get one. It was pretty obvious he was there, and anyway, what she'd said hadn't been a question. He wasn't answering questions which weren't questions. He'd been caught like that enough times.

"Well, come on in and make yourself at home. I thought we'd have tea out here in the kitchen, to be more cozy. Your great-uncle's having a bit of a rest—he always has a little rest-up between three and half past four, does Mr. Greville, come rain or shine, and always the better man for it afterwards, that's what I say. And I told him I'd be happy to look after you, so we could have the chance to get to know each other a bit—if you can make do with my company, that is? . . . Yes, well there now. You can wash your hands over at the sink if you like, to save going upstairs. I've put a towel all ready."

James did as he was told, glad of the chance to turn his back. But he could feel her eyes on it. He made the washing operation last as long as he could. Under the cold tap, his palm stopped bleeding.

"There, now come and sit yourself down."

He sat down, trying not to look at the stuff on the table. Currant bread, and hot scones with butter. He hadn't eaten since he'd left London. He looked at the kitchen instead.

Vast, with copper things hanging in rows, and blue and white plates on a dresser—

"Well, so here we are." She had sat down now, too, on the opposite chair. "You just go ahead and help yourself."

"I'm not hungry, thanks."

"Not . . .? But I thought, with that long drive from London . . . You could surely manage just one scone, couldn't you? I made them specially."

"No thanks."

"Oh please try. Just put one on your plate. It might tempt you."

He felt her eyes on him again, on the side of his face. Then she fussed with the teapot.

"A cup of tea first, then?"

He could allow himself that much. "Thanks."

He took the tea from her and sipped it slowly. He wondered how long it would be before she came out with more questions. Her hands were fidgeting with her empty plate. The butter on the scones had begun to congeal now, but she didn't take one.

"You look a bit dusty. I expect you've been having an explore round, have you?"

"Not really."

"It's . . . it's a lovely old garden. And the house, too. I always think how lucky I am to be able to live here. Of course, I've been here for nearly as long as I can remember, so I'm probably not the best judge really. You do like what you've seen of it so far, don't you?"

"It's OK."

"Oh, good. You can call me Sarah, by the way, if you'd like to. Everybody else does."

"Thanks."

"Yes, such a great big place for us two oldies, I always think. But it's been like that for years and years now, just

Mr. Greville and me, so I suppose I've got used to it. We all get used to things in time, don't we? Though it's always a bit hard at the beginning, I expect, getting used to new people and places and everything. You . . . you've always lived in London, have you?"

"Yes."

"I expect this all seems very strange and different then, doesn't it?"

"I hadn't really thought."

"No . . . well, that's the best way, isn't it, when all's said and done. Doesn't do to think too much, life still goes on the same. Perhaps you could tell me a bit about London and your flat there and everything? It doesn't have to be now, of course—any time will do. But I'd enjoy hearing all about it. I don't get much opportunity of meeting many new people out here in the country so it'll be a real treat for me, having a fresh face round the old place. D'you know, I've never been to London in all my life. I expect that surprises you, doesn't it?"

"Not really."

"No. Well, I'm sure there's *something* you'd like to tell me about yourself, isn't there? To help me to get to know you?"

"There is one thing."

"Yes?"

"I'm thirteen now."

"I . . . I'm sorry?"

"I'm thirteen. I thought maybe you hadn't realized."

"Oh . . . oh yes, I'm sure I . . . Well, here's me talking away and you sitting there with an empty cup. I'll just put a drop more water in the pot."

From the corner of his eye he watched her move away to the stove. Small and gray-haired, with the kind sort of face that social workers had. He didn't trust kind faces, he'd seen too many of them. They were the ones who caught you off your guard. Nice cozy chat over tea, all written up in a file later on—

"There we are."

"Thanks."

"You can get to know the house after tea if you want to. Your great-uncle would like that, he so much wants you to feel at home here. And you'll be able to tell him what you think of it all later on, when you see him. Half past five, he said, so that gives you plenty of time. You're pleased with your room, are you?"

"It's fine, thanks."

"I . . . I looked for your bag earlier on, to unpack a bit for you. But I couldn't seem to find it."

"That's OK." He resisted the temptation to feel in his pocket, to make sure that the key of the wardrobe was there. "I've put it away."

"Oh . . . well, you're nicely settled in then. If you've got any dirty things that need washing, you've only to let me have them and—"

"Thanks."

The kitchen clock ticked loudly. A drowsy bee bumped and bumped against the window, trying to get out. He listened to it, knowing how it felt.

"It's things like that—the bits of washing and everything—that are always the hardest to get used to when you come to a new place, isn't it? But you can trust me to cope with all the little jobs your mother used to do for you, can't you?"

"Thanks. She didn't, though."

"Didn't . . . ? I'm not quite sure I . . ."

"Didn't do them. She couldn't cope with washing."

"No. No, of course not." Her hands had left the plate now, and dropped down to her lap. She was twiddling with her apron. "I was so sorry to hear she's poorly, James. But at least she's in good hands now, in the hospital, so it's—"

"She's not poorly. She's being dried out."

"I . . ."

"She's an alco. She's being dried out."

He thought of her there. He'd been there the first time, to see her. He'd sat by her bed with the chocolate he'd brought, but she hadn't woken up. This was the fourth time. It wasn't worth bothering now. "Didn't they tell you, then—about her being an alco?"

"Well, yes I . . . I think it was probably mentioned. I think the Supervising Officer—"

"The what?"

"The Supervising Officer, earlier on. He seemed such a nice man."

"Oh, Probation Officer, you mean."

"James, you're not on probation, you mustn't say that. He explained about it. You're only on what he called a Supervision Order."

"Amounts to the same thing, doesn't it?"

"No, of course it doesn't, it's—"

"You know all about these things then, do you?"

"Well, no . . . I . . ."

Her voice trailed away. James sensed her helplessness and was glad of it. He treated himself to a scone, and tossed it up and down in his hand: to show her, not that he wanted it, but that he'd won it.

"I think I'll be going to my room now, then, if that's all."

"Yes. Yes, of course."

"Thanks for tea."

He got up from his chair and put it neatly against the table. She didn't raise her eyes towards him. He left her looking down at her empty plate.

4

James sat by his bedroom window, eating the scone. Across the tiny dry wound in the flat of his palm, the dart rolled backwards and forwards catching the sunlight, silver and scarlet. He watched it, feeling its balance inside him. Feathers and steel, and hand and eye. It was beautiful.

He finished the scone and put the dart back in his bag in the wardrobe. He was still hungry.

He chewed at his thumbnail. Which, he decided, was likely to be all he was going to get for the rest of the day. There would probably be supper some time, but he wasn't intending to eat it. He'd not touch a thing until breakfast. By then he'd have made his point.

There was always the village . . .

Some hope. From what he'd glimpsed of it earlier on, it hardly looked likely to run to a fast-food place. And nor for that matter did his pocket. He had one pound twenty-five pence. And that was for later, emergencies only. The one last bit of his independence, in case he decided to leave. Which meant sixteen hours without food.

A sound from the garden made him go back to the window.

The Sarah-woman must have left the kitchen not long after he had. She was already down on one of the lawns, beheading the roses. In the breathless air he could hear the snip snip snip. Perhaps to relieve her feelings. She ought to have tried a chain saw.

He listened. He'd rather it *had* been a chain saw, it would have been more noisy. There was something about the sound of the scissors that gave him a sense of the creeps. He wondered why. And then he suddenly remembered a rhyme from when he was younger. It used to be his favorite, because it scared him half to death.

> *The great tall tailor always comes*
> *To little boys who suck their thumbs,*
> *And ere they dream what he's about,*
> *He takes his great sharp scissors out . . .*

The same sound now, and the same rhythm, tap-tap-tapping across the lawn. No wonder he used to wake up screaming.

"*Highly impressionable.*"

He spoke the words aloud. He'd seen them in his file last week, when the bloke had left the room to make a phone call. Probably some fancy way of saying that he still had nightmares now.

> *The door flew open, in he ran,*
> *The great, long, red-legg'd scissor-man.*
> *Snip! snap! snip! the scissors go;*
> *And Conrad cries out "Oh! oh! oh!"*
> *Snip! snap! snip! They go so fast,*
> *That both his thumbs are off at last.*

It must be years since he'd heard it. Why had it waited till today, then, and not come back to him through all those years in London? Perhaps it was the noise there, the traffic and the music, and the people always talking. The noise had made a kind of wall to shut remembering out. But here it was all different, there was nothing but the silence. The present here was empty: there was more room for the past.

He went back to the chewing of his thumbnail and listened to the scissors. Then he quickly whipped his thumb out of his mouth. Better to be safe than sorry.

"Crazy."

He snorted, half-ashamed.

"Enough to turn anybody barmy, this place is."

Then a new thought struck him. If the Sarah-woman was out there in the garden . . . He got up and left the room.

The house was quiet. He went down the two flights of stairs and arrived in the ground-floor hallway. He looked at his watch. *Three till four-thirty, come rain or shine*, she'd said. So his great-uncle would still be resting. The coast was clear.

The kitchen table was just as he'd left it. He took four of the scones and dropped them inside his T-shirt, then arranged the others to cover their traces. A currant-bread sandwich of plum jam and sugar. And he was back at his window in three and a half minutes flat.

"Better luck next time, scissor-woman."

He grinned through a mouthful of breadcrumbs, and made the thumbs-up at her stooping back.

She was still out there in the garden, and it wasn't half past four yet. OK, she'd told him to get to know the house, so he would. There was nothing else on offer before the star attraction at five-thirty, the session with his great-uncle—and, anyway, he was a great believer in getting his bearings. It might come in handy.

He brushed the telltale crumbs from the sill of his bedroom, then went back down to the ground-floor hallway. Just as upstairs on the two other floors, a corridor ran the whole length of the house dividing it roughly in two equal parts. Down here, the dining room, pantries and kitchen made up the back part. The two larger rooms at the front of the house, with an entrance hall running between them, must be the best ones. Which probably meant his great-uncle's . . .

He tiptoed along the front hall he'd come in by when first he'd arrived here, and stopped halfway along it. A door on his left, and a door on his right. He listened. From the door on his right he could just catch the sound of low wheezing. He opened the door on his left.

He was surprised. It must be his great-uncle's bedroom, with a bathroom built on at one side. So, two useful pieces of info: first, the old bloke took his afternoon nap in his study; second, he must have some trouble in getting up-stairs. James nodded. The second fact cheered him: it meant that his own room, two floors above this, was out of the old man's reach.

He glanced round the bedroom and took in its details. White walls, an iron-framed bed, an old buttoned chair by the window. A black wooden cross on the wall by the bedside. Medicine bottles and books.

"Creepy."

He closed the door.

He listened again to the snip-snip-snipping, then tiptoed away upstairs.

The first floor was Sarah's. A large room at the front of the house, over what must be his great-uncle's study, was clearly her sitting room and bedroom rolled into one. It was all that the old man's wasn't: cozy and flowery and cluttered with knickknacks. On the rest of this floor, only unused bedrooms, a couple of boxrooms, a white-tiled bathroom and loo.

He went up again, to the floor which contained his own

bedroom. The same as below. Apart from his bedroom and bathroom, the place wasn't used now. It was like a museum, just bits of the past covered up and forgotten. Smelly old curtains in brown cardboard boxes. Copper and brass things wrapped up in blankets. Armchairs and sofas in dusty gray sheeting, like lumpy old women in shrouds. He didn't disturb them.

The corridor ended. He leaned back against the wall.

"What. A. Lousy. Dump."

Still, it could have been worse, he supposed. At least he knew now that he had the top floor to himself. At least he was private. So that was all right. All right now, anyway, in the afternoon sunlight. He tried not to think of tonight.

Well, apart from the last narrow staircase, here on his left in the corner, he'd finished casing the place. He glanced at his watch, and climbed up.

The door at the top was stiff with disuse. He pushed it half-open.

Dust rose and spiraled in thin blades of sunlight through gaps in the roof-tiles. He stared round and gave a long whistle. The dust spiraled faster.

"What *have* we got here, then?"

The attic. Water-tanks lagged with black cobwebs. Joists leading off into darkness, crusty with droppings and straw. He edged his way slowly along them. After a minute he paused.

He looked back, gauging the distance he'd covered: a long way already, he must have crossed half of the house. It was hardly worth going on farther, there was nothing up here but old heat and old shadows. At least, he hoped that there wasn't: he'd lost sight of his only way out.

"No thumb-sucking up here, mate. You wouldn't stand a chance."

He stood undecided, then turned and went on.

The tiles in this half were sounder, the needles of sunlight less frequent. This must be the side of the house that was nearest the derelict garden, the side that contained his own bedroom. Perhaps, even now, he was walking directly above it—

He halted again. He had reached what must be a partition: a door in a solid brick wall. He tried it. Locked? Or just jammed?

"If it's locked, it must mean there's something worth seeing behind it."

Either way, he could probably budge it. The timber felt rotten enough.

Inch by inch, the door shifted outward. Sunlight broke in through a tearing of stems. It was only the ivy that saved him. The attic had ended abruptly: there was nothing beyond but a forty-foot drop to the disused garden, straight through the boughs of the oak.

He crouched down low. Holding his breath he peered out again through the chinks in the creepers, as hidden as if he was lying in ambush. Ambush . . . A dark and secret excitement throbbed through him. Then, slowly, he smiled. Not three yards below him, the blackbird had settled. For a long time he watched it, unseen.

5

Just gone five-thirty.

James paused in front of the door, listening. There was no sound from within. He didn't have to go through with this if he didn't want to. His bag was still packed upstairs in the wardrobe, he could fetch it down and clear off with nobody knowing, hitch a lift back to London. Not back to the flat, though: that'd be the first place they'd look. But there were other places, where mates of his had told him he'd make money . . . He chewed his lip, uncertain. Then he cursed himself under his breath, and knocked.

There was a moment's silence.

"Come in."

The study was broad and high, and smelt of lavender polish and leathery books. In the window recess, his great-uncle sat at a desk. He was writing.

"Oh, James. Good." A thin attempt at a smile twitched at the corners of his mouth for an instant, then gave up the ghost. "Do close the door and have a seat. I won't be a moment." His eyes went back to his pen.

James sat down in the chair he'd been shown, on the opposite side of the desk. He glanced across at the half-lowered head. Bone-gray hair, and bone-gray face. Scrawny black suit. The walking canes were hooked on the edge of the chair arm.

James's nervousness left him. A sense of defiance came in its place, tying a knot in his stomach. It was clear what was up: the old man was trying to scare him. Well, he'd have to try harder. James was an old hand at *this* game. He'd spent half of his life on the other side of a desk.

He looked away. The room was all books, layer after layer, rich dark brown to the ceiling. And the ceiling was knobbly with white plaster flowers and leaves, like icing. He waited. Like being inside a Christmas cake, with the knife about to come in.

"There, now."

He tensed and turned back. The cap was being neatly screwed on the pen. Then the pen was laid down on the paper. James wondered for a moment if the writing had been about him.

"Well, James, so here you are then, at Greville Lodge." The voice didn't sound enthusiastic. It was thin and tired, like the face. "I trust you are beginning to find your way around?"

"Yes thanks."

"It must all seem very strange to begin with." He felt the old man's eyes resting on him, then sink again to the desk-top. "But I am sure that you will appreciate, too, that it is all very strange for us as well, for Sarah and for me. You have no doubt gathered already that we live a very quiet life here, and clearly we shall have to be prepared to make some adjustments. But, equally, you must be prepared to make some adjustments too if the experiment is to be a success."

He spoke slowly, as if repeating something rehearsed. Perhaps it was all written down on that paper—

"We mustn't forget, of course, that it *is* only an experiment, for these fourteen days initially, and that both we and you are free to admit at any time that it hasn't worked out satisfactorily. Needless to say, I hope that it will work out. I trust you feel the same?"

"Yes."

"Good. I thought it best to clear up the point before we go any farther. And now perhaps we had also better begin by trying to be clear in our minds what the exact situation is."

His hand reached across to the side of the desk and drew a typewritten sheet towards him. He looked at it with something like distaste.

"I am sure that it seems unnecessary to you to go over things in this way, but I think it advisable for both our sakes. As I said, I have always lived a very sheltered life here, so you must realize that problems of this kind are something of which I have had no experience before."

Lucky bloody you. James gazed out of the window, where the lawns and the drive stretched away. He shouldn't have come in here. He should have gone, fetched his bag and gone. He'd have been out there by now, down the drive and on the main road. Maybe already in a truck—

"So, as I read the situation, James, you have received several . . . several legal cautions over the past two or three years, but for one reason or another you have seen fit to ignore them. That is so, is it not?"

"I suppose so."

"If you had been older, the result would have been probation. But as you are still only thirteen, you have been placed on what is termed a Supervision Order, under the charge of the . . . the Social Services."

He mouthed the words as if he were chewing ashes.

"Under the circumstances, James, I feel I perhaps have the right to ask you a question which has troubled me. Why have you been . . . been stealing things? You realized, I am sure, that it was a criminal offense and . . . and a sin? Did you need to take these things? Were you lacking for anything? . . . It would be more helpful if you could answer. Did you need money?"

"Not really."

"So there was no reason?"

"Not really."

"No. Well, as matters rest, then, I am told that you will have to report next week to the Supervising Officer who brought you here today, and again at regular intervals after that. And also that you will be obliged to begin some kind of . . . of group therapy in a fortnight's time. I am afraid I am not quite sure what that is. Do you know?"

"I.T."

"I'm sorry?"

"Intermediate Treatment."

"Yes, well as long as you understand. I suppose what it finally boils down to is that—given your home situation—there was the real possibility of your being . . . being sent to a foster family."

"Taken into Care."

"Yes. As you say. Taken into Care." He chewed on more ashes. With any luck, they'd choke him. "You are no doubt aware that there has been no contact between me and your . . . your family for many years now, so you can appreciate that it all came as something of a shock when I was informed of what had happened, and of what would certainly happen next if I felt unable to take you in here. I want you to understand that, if I had been here alone, there would have been no question of it. You owe this experiment to Sarah."

"I'm grateful."

"I am sure that you will show her so. Well, James, that is the situation as it has been presented to me. Would you say that it gives a fair picture of what has happened?"

"Seems OK."

"Good. All that remains, then, is for all of us to do what we can to get through the next fortnight as successfully as possible. After that . . ." The unsmiling voice paused for a moment, then seemed abruptly to change direction. "Have you seen anything of your father at all?"

"What?"

"Your father, James. Have you seen anything of him?"

"How should I know?"

"I am not sure that that kind of answer is quite what I was hoping for. I asked you if you had seen your father."

"I told you. I might have. I don't know, do I?"

"What do you mean—you don't know?"

"I don't know which one he was. There were too many to choose from."

There was a silence. James waited. The old man didn't raise his eyes.

"I see. Then there seems little to hope for in that direction. So we shall have to make the best of the situation as it stands for the time being and see how things develop, shall we not?"

"I suppose so."

"James, you do realize, don't you, that there is not a great deal of hope for my niece?"

James felt suddenly unreal. The words had seemed entirely unconnected, with him or with his life or with anything about him, like a bit of conversation overheard at a bus stop.

"Your . . . your niece?"

"I understand that her condition has been deteriorating for some time."

"What . . . what d'you mean, your niece?"

"We have not, as I said, been in contact for many years, but I have been told that her liver is now badly affected."

"You mean my mother, don't you?"

"I am sure that the doctors will do all they think necessary to—"

"You mean my *mother*."

"Yes . . . your mother."

For one appalling moment James thought he was going to cry. He clenched his hands in his lap to make the nails dig into the flesh, and tightened the knot of defiance inside him. Then he shrugged.

"It's OK," he said. "I know."

"I realize that it must be very painful for you."

"No. Not really. I never saw much of her anyway. She was out most of the time."

"I see. I'm sorry."

"Yes. Can I go now?"

"While you are here, Sarah will see to everything you want. You have only to ask—"

"Can I go now?"

"Of course. You will no doubt be wanting to settle in."

James got to his feet and moved away. With his hand on the doorknob he paused without turning his head as the voice came again.

"James, I . . . I hope you will be happy here."

"Thanks."

He closed the door behind him.

6

The blackbird sang from the bough. The earth and sky sang back. No sign of the boy, no tracks across the garden, only a rustle in the shadowed ivy, high in the wall where no boy could come. The bird sang on.

Death came with a whistle, in a flash of steel sunlight. Feathers towards feathers, the red towards the black. The spike bit home, through the eye that turned to meet it. And the singing and the earth and sky were gone.

7

James came out of the bathroom and stood for a moment in the corridor outside his room. It was dark now.

Supper had been hell. He'd sat in front of the shepherd's pie and managed not to eat it. The Sarah-woman had hardly stopped talking, and his great-uncle had hardly started. Secretly, they'd both watched him.

He'd been glad to escape, to come up to bed on his own. But now he wasn't so sure.

He listened for traffic: for any sound to tell him he wasn't alone here. But there was nothing. He'd left his Walkman behind in London and he wished now that he'd brought it, even though it was broken. The headphones might have stopped this creepy silence from pressing so hard on his ears. More silence than he could ever remember hearing. The house was dead—or dying: just breathing a bit now and then through the wheeze of a water pipe, the creak of a floorboard.

Why were they creaking, anyway? There wasn't anyone up here. He looked down the shadowy passage.

His great-grandparents must have been here once. They'd probably stood on this very spot where he was standing now. And his grandfather too—his great-uncle's younger brother, Edward—who'd been killed with his wife in a car crash. But James had only been two when they'd died, so he wouldn't know them even if they suddenly came walking towards him, creaking across the boards. . . . He shivered.

"Barmy. Dead and done for, that's what *they* are. Ought to think themselves lucky. Who'd want to come back to this place once they'd got shot of it? And there aren't such things as ghosts, anyway."

But maybe ghosts weren't like that, really: not people walking about with their heads stuck under their armpits. Maybe ghosts weren't things that people turned into after they'd died, but things they'd left behind from when they'd been alive: all the things they'd once said to each other, all the feelings they'd had when they'd been here—maybe those were the kinds of things that were all still here somehow, like dust in the cracks of the floorboards, even though the people who'd said them and felt them were gone now.

"Truly barmy."

He'd be getting his nightmares if he went on like this. Sleepwalking again. And he didn't fancy sleepwalking round a place like this.

He turned quickly away and went into his room.

He stood there for a while, with his back to the door. This had always been the worst moment, the closing of the bedroom door. It meant that the night had really started. Daytime was OK, he could just about cope with things in the daylight. But he dreaded the nighttime, and going to sleep. Things were out of his control then. And here it was even worse than at home.

Half-ashamed of himself, he went through his usual nightly routine, checking for things that might crawl out of hiding the minute he'd switched off the light. Inside the wardrobe, under the bed, behind the back of the armchair. It was all OK.

He undressed slowly, eyeing the room as he did so. He felt uneasy, taking his clothes off with it watching. They didn't know each other yet.

In his pajamas he went across to the window. There was no moon, only a single blade of light from his great-uncle's bedroom, cutting a slice from the garden. It stretched out over the terrace and driveway, and ended up on the edge of the lawn. Its left-hand side just touched the hedge of the disused garden.

The thought of the garden made James draw back. He looked at the ceiling. Today he'd been up there, walking across the attic to a door that led nowhere, in the end wall of the house. And he'd returned there later, after he'd seen his great-uncle. . . . The thing had been dead before it hit the ground. He'd had a job getting the dart out.

"Served it right, anyway."

Paying life back, it was called. First installment.

He went to his bed and pulled back the sheets. They smelled clean, like soap-flakes. They made him aware that his pajamas were filthy. So what. Maybe he'd try and wash them tomorrow, in the bathroom. He'd done it often enough at home. He wasn't going to let *her* see them and turn her nose up

His hands touched warm rubber. He cursed. What right had she got, coming in here without asking? And how old did she reckon he was? He threw the hot-water bottle onto the floor.

Soon, now, he was going to have to switch out the light, get into bed. Then he'd go to sleep and the things in his head would wake up—

A sudden footstep on the staircase made him clamber in under the blanket, half-angry, half-relieved.

There was a knock at his door.

"Can I come in, James?"

"Yes."

It was her, the Sarah-woman. She was holding a tray.

"I just thought I'd pop up and make sure you'd got everything you wanted. I . . . I've brought you a glass of milk and some biscuits."

"Thanks."

"I'm sorry you didn't fancy the bit of pie I did tonight. It's hard for me, not knowing the sort of things you like yet. You've only got to tell me—if there's anything special I can do for you, I'll be ever so happy to try and—"

"That's OK, thanks."

"Oh well, at least the milk and biscuits will help till the morning. Now, you're sure you'll be warm enough?"

"I'll be OK."

He turned on his side, away from her. He could see her reflection in the wardrobe. He had the sudden uneasy feeling that she wanted to tuck him in.

"Well, if you're sure you're all right, I'd better be making tracks to bed myself, I suppose." But she made no movement to go. "Your great-uncle's turned in for the night already. He always goes early. Not that he sleeps much, just dozes half the night in that old armchair of his by the window. So there's nothing else I can be getting you, then? You're all nice and settled?"

"Yes."

"Well, there then. I'm pleased. The first night in a new place always seems a bit strange, I expect, doesn't it? But it's a friendly enough old house when you get to know it. And . . . and I'm only close by, just downstairs."

He wondered what she was trying to say. With a terrible sinking of his stomach, he thought he knew.

"If you should need anything—"

"I won't, thanks."

"I'll leave the passageway light on, shall I?"

"You needn't bother."

"I just thought . . ."

"I'm going to get some sleep now, if that's OK."

"Yes. I'm sure you'll have a good night. But you needn't be afraid of waking me up if . . . well, if you should have a bit of a dream or something."

He'd been right, then. They'd gone and told her all about him. Every last bloody thing.

"What d'you mean, dream?"

"Oh, James, you know what I mean. These nightmares . . ."

"What nightmares?"

"I'm sorry, I didn't mean to pry—"

"That's OK. What nightmares?"

"It was just that they said—"

"Been talking about me, have they? Making things up?"

"No, of course they haven't."

"Well, that's all right then, isn't it?"

Her reflection hovered, at a loss. Then it turned and moved slowly across to the door.

"Good night then, James. I hope you sleep well."

He didn't answer.

Her footsteps creaked away down the stairs.

He leapt out of bed and stayed by the door for a while, with his ear pressed to the panel. She'd gone to her own room now and wouldn't come back. He was alone.

He switched off the light and stood for a moment, frozen in darkness. Then he went across to the wardrobe and fumbled about for his bag. He found what he wanted, clean again now and safe in its box, under his few bits of clothing. Clutching it to him, he got into bed.

They'd never find out. They'd found out everything else about him, his stealing and sleepwalks and nightmares, till he'd got nothing personal left. Except this, his only secret, and his only protection. He slipped his fingers in under the lid and stroked it gently, steel and feathers. It had been from his mother, on his tenth birthday, the last present she'd ever bought.

8

James woke up in pitch darkness. He didn't know where he was. His pajama jacket was icy with sweat.

He'd been dreaming. He'd been on his own in a silent black room and a noise had come, scratching its way towards him. Then silence again. But he'd known that whatever it was was still there, somewhere near him, waiting. Then a new sound had come—

He shrank back in his pillow.

It had come again now, from outside his window. He tunneled back under the bedclothes, dragging the pillow down after. But the sound was still out there. The song of a blackbird. Then only the silence, and a light scratch of footsteps on gravel, quietly moving away.

9

"Are there any animals or birds or anything round here at night?"

Sarah turned towards James from the stove. She looked slightly surprised. But whether surprised by the question itself, or by the fact that he'd asked her a question at all, he couldn't be sure.

"Oh, well now, we do get a fox now and then. And hedgehogs sometimes. There was a badger once, too, out on the lawn, but they're shy old things as a rule, badgers."

She came across to the kitchen table with a plate of bacon and eggs. James began to eat, trying not to look hungry.

"No birds, then?" he said.

"Well, the usual ones. Owls, mainly. A real old racket they make sometimes, down in the copse. Always sad they sound to me. But there, I expect it's just their way."

"What about blackbirds and things?"

"Blackbirds? Well, in the daytime there are, of course. Finches too, and wagtails. But not at night. Day-birds, blackbirds are. You're interested in nature then, are you, James? Bird-watching and suchlike?"

"Not really."

"No. But I expect you've got a nice lot of birds in London too, haven't you?"

"Yes. Sparrows."

He felt her watch him for a moment, uncertain. Then she went away to the sink.

So it was all right, then. Just part of his dream. He hadn't really woken up, only dreamt he had. He often did that. And anyway, even if this place was weird enough to make him almost start believing that dead people turned into ghosts, he certainly wasn't going to start believing that birds did. He might be *highly impressionable*, but he wasn't completely cracked.

Which only left the problem of what he was going to do with himself this morning. Get out of the house, for a start. Maybe down to the village—

She was back again. "I can do you a bit more bacon if you'd like it. There's plenty in the fridge."

"No thanks."

"Still, it's a real treat to see I've found something you fancy, anyway. I was getting quite worried. And there's nothing like a good breakfast to set you up for the day, I always say. I only wish Mr. Greville would eat a bit more. One slice of toast at eight o'clock and that's him done, then off to his study till lunchtime. Oh, he said to say good morning to you, specially, and if there's anything you want you're to let him know."

"Thanks."

"And he hoped you slept well, your first night. You . . . you did sleep all right, didn't you?"

"Course."

"I'm so glad. I really am."

She didn't have to say what she was thinking. She had nightmares written all over her face. James felt his hackles rising again. He finished his breakfast in silence.

It was Sarah herself who solved the problem of the morning, just as he was leaving the kitchen.

"Oh, James, I was wondering if you might like to pop down to the village for me? You don't have to, I can always go myself, but I just thought you might like a look around and—"

"OK."

"Oh. That is kind of you, and it's only three or four things. Now, where have I put it? Yes, here we are. I've made you a list, with the name of the shop to go to. It's only the Stores, so you can't miss it, and this five-pound note should cover everything. If you could just remember to jot down the prices . . ." She faltered. A little crimson rash crept from under her collar and up to her ear. "Or rather . . . no, don't you bother about that, it's—"

"That's OK, it's no bother. I'll jot down the prices all right. We don't want to go and get ourselves shortchanged, do we?"

He took the list from her, and left the room.

The village was puny. He'd almost walked through it before he'd realized he'd got there. Cottages, a church, a pub, three shops and a duck pond.

"Just great."

He felt exposed. As he went by, the villagers stopped talking and eyed him, nodding and smiling. He wondered if they'd been told all about him, along with everyone else. It wouldn't have surprised him. Oh well, he hoped it gave them a thrill. They could certainly use one, in this place. On reflection, though, he decided that it wasn't very likely that they *did* know. Mr.-God-Almighty-Greville wouldn't have gone out of his way to advertise he had a dropout as an inmate.

James found the Stores and looked through the doorway. Self-service, so that was all right. He waited outside, pretending to study the Special Offer stickers glued to the windows. Two customers came out, which left one still remaining. He opened the door and went in.

On his right, with the usual tall plastic rack for displaying cigarettes, was the cash-desk. An overlarge woman in a green nylon tunic was perched up beside it, like a frog on a toadstool.

"Good morning, dear."

"Morning."

He took a wire basket and made for the shelves. For a couple of minutes he wandered around them, sizing things up with a practiced eye. The strawberry jam looked like being the answer. There were only two jars of that.

The other customer went to the cash-desk.

OK, then. Two jars of jam into the basket, one bag of sugar into the basket, one tin of custard into the basket, one box of matches into the pocket, two jars of jam back on the shelf.

He went across to the till and waited his turn.

"Now then, dear, you've found everything you were wanting, have you?"

"I haven't, actually. I couldn't see the strawberry jam."

"It's down at the far end with the other flavors, next to the sugar."

"I looked there."

"Well, I know we've got some."

She plopped off her toadstool and moved across to the shelf.

Leaning back against the edge of the counter, hands behind him, James watched her. She came back, pleased with herself.

"Here we are, dear, I knew we had. Somebody must have picked it up and put it back in the wrong place. That's the trouble with all this self-service business—I could always be sure things stayed where I put them in the old days."

James gave her a grin of agreement. He paid, and left the shop.

This was his favorite moment: it was always the best part, not knowing what you'd got until after. Behind-the-back shopping, he called it. He risked a look in his pockets. Not bad, really. Could have been worse, considering the lousy selection. A pack of Dunhills, and a pack of Players, no filter.

He sat with his shopping bag, up on the churchyard wall at the top of a rough grassy bank by the high street, carving his initials in the stone with the spike of his dart and smoking a cigarette.

He felt better now, more sure of himself. More real, somehow. He hadn't needed the cigarettes, he didn't even like them. But he'd needed to take them. He'd got something of his own again, that he'd won by himself, for himself. And they hadn't caught him.

"What a cinch. These poor suckers up here wouldn't last a day in London. They'd be eaten alive."

He completed the *J* and the *E* and set to work on the *G* for Greville. His mother had kept her maiden name, for obvious reasons. He wondered how she was, and if she'd ever wake up enough to think about how he was doing. *James, you do realize, don't you, that there is not a great deal of hope for my niece?* He gouged harder at the G. It didn't make any odds, anyhow. He didn't need her, or anybody. He was OK.

He sat back and considered his handiwork. It looked good. J. E. G. had made his mark.

"James. Edward. Greville."

His mouth twisted in a sudden bitter grin. If she didn't come round, if she pegged it, there'd only be two Grevilles left. After all those years and years of them up at Greville Lodge, just two left. And what a classic pair. A cranky old cripple who'd never even got married, and a thirteen-year-old social case with a criminal record. God had certainly done himself proud this time—

"Hey, you!"

The voice made James jump. He looked down the bank. A bald old man in baggy corduroy trousers was glaring up at him.

"What're you doing up there?"

"What's it look like?"

"Don't you talk to me that way, lad. Dropping paper all over the place, that's what it looks like. And what d'you think you're doing with that dart?"

"A bit of stone carving, thanks."

"Well, pack it in."

"I just have. I've finished it now. Anyway, it's nothing to lose your hair about." He pointed across to the gravestones. "It's the in-thing round here, in case you hadn't noticed."

"And you can pack that smoking in while you're about it, a kid of your age. I'll be telling your father when I meet him."

"You do that. And while you're about it, you can tell him I'd like to meet him myself."

"You just clear off out of it, you cheeky young beggar. I'll have the police on you if I catch you again."

The man went off, mumbling. James called after him.

"Hey, by the way, mate, mind how you go, won't you? The natives round here aren't very friendly."

He watched the receding back and felt a sudden vicious urge to hurl the dart at it. Then the feeling reminded him of the last time he'd hurled it, and brought a new thought to him. He frowned, tapping his lip with the spike. There was something he needed to investigate, up at the Lodge.

10

"For what we have received, may God be praised and blessed."

Mr. Greville fell silent, presumably waiting for praise and blessing. Sarah said amen. James didn't. It was creepy. And he'd only received salad, anyway.

"I'll bring some coffee to the study for you, shall I?"

"Thank you, Sarah. That would be most kind."

James watched the old man hoist himself up from his chair at the lunch table and make his way stiffly to the dining room door, like an insect on sticks. Stick-insect. James grinned to himself.

The door closed.

"Poor thing," Sarah said.

She began to clear the table.

"Well, James, you've got something nice planned for this afternoon, have you? A walk maybe? There're some nice walks round here."

"I'll be OK."

"Not but that this weather's a bit hot for walking, I must say. It's the insects I don't like, always the same in August. If you'd rather stay indoors, there're a lot of books you could read. A proper old place for books this is, and no mistake. I'm sure your great-uncle won't mind you helping yourself to anything that takes your fancy—except in his study, of course. You'd have to ask if you wanted any of those."

"Why?"

"Well, it's his collection in there. Valuable, some of them are: seventeenth century, he says. Almost afraid to dust them I am, sometimes. Oh yes, thinks the world of his books does Mr. Greville. Morning, afternoon and night it is with him—reading, and making his catalogues, and working out dates and things." She sighed. "Like children to him, they are. Of course, if you were to be interested in seeing them, I know it would make him ever so happy to show them to you. He doesn't get a lot of chance of—"

"I've brought my own paperback. I don't do much reading, anyhow."

"No. Well, I prefer a good paperback myself, I must admit, when I've got the time. I tell you what, though—you could always watch a bit of television if you fancy it."

"T. V.? Where?"

"Up in my room. It's only a little portable with one of those indoor aerials, so it's not a very good picture, but you'd be ever so welcome. So long as you don't turn it up too loud, that's all—your great-uncle isn't a great one for the telly."

James hesitated, and cursed himself for letting her notice.

"No thanks," he said.

"You are welcome, really you are. I can see you'd like it, and I don't watch it much myself."

"I've got loads to do, thanks."

She sighed again. "Oh well, I'll be getting on, then, and leaving you to it."

James waited. Her footsteps clicked away along the flagstones of the passage. In the kitchen, water splashed on dishes. He left the dining room and went up to the top floor of the house.

In the attic, the noonday heat was as thick as ever. He edged his way through it. A bee had come in through a gap in the roof-tiles and was blundering about in a cage of barred sunlight. James was glad of its presence. It was better than being alone.

He reached the end wall and pushed the door open as far as he could through the tangle of stems. Flat on his stomach he eased himself forward, bracing himself with his hands on the doorposts. His head and shoulders came clear of the creepers. He looked down the vertical drop. For a minute he probed in the thick growths of ivy, then changed his position and tried squinting up at the tip of the gable. But neither above nor below could he find any sign to show why the door should be there.

"Unless they had it put here specially for me, banking on me finding it and walking straight through it. Or *sleep*walking through it . . ."

He shuddered and drew himself in.

For a while he stayed there, thinking. It seemed pretty clear that the door wasn't used now. But it was equally clear that it must have been used at some time or other, or it wouldn't have been there. But why in the end wall, leading to nowhere?

"And why just up here in the attic of all crazy places?"

If it *was* just up here. But maybe it wasn't. Maybe there were three other mystery doors directly below this, down on the three lower floors.

He got to his feet and crept quietly away.

Back on his own floor, he examined the corridor wall that bordered the derelict garden. It was sealed by an eight-foot bookcase, screwed solidly into the brickwork. The screws were rusty with age.

He went down again.

The same on this floor: another great corridor bookcase screwed up against the end wall . . .

There *might* be other doors, then, vertically in line with the one in the attic. But, if so, they'd been hidden from view now. He could try the ground floor and see if it followed the same sort of pattern: the corridor wall, to the right at the foot of the stairs. He couldn't remember seeing a bookcase, but there might be one there all the same.

He paused before he reached the hall, and listened. At the farther end, the clink of dishes meant that Sarah was still busy. He made his way on down.

"Of *course*."

He recognized it the moment he saw it. He'd passed by it a hundred times already without a glance in its direction. Not a bookcase, but a long dark velvet curtain with wooden rings that held it to a pole.

He found the door behind it. Oak-paneled, with a tarnished brass handle. He tried it. It was locked.

He hadn't heard the footsteps.

"Are you looking for something, James?"

James let the curtain go and turned round quickly. His great-uncle was behind him, on his sticks.

"What?"

"I asked if you were looking for something."

"No. Not really."

"I'm sorry if I startled you."

"You didn't."

"It pleases me that you are getting to know the house. It must all seem a little forbidding at first, but I have grown very fond of it." He looked round at it slowly, but not at the curtain. "Though perhaps I am overfond in my view of it. Do you think I am?"

"I . . . I don't know really."

"I get about very little now, so I no longer see a great deal of the place. Parts of it are possibly very different from my memory of them. It may be that I still tend to see it as it used to be, rather than as it is now. But your room and bathroom are satisfactory, I trust?"

"Yes."

"Good. Good. And you have already visited the garden, I think?"

"Some of it."

"It's many years since I can claim to have seen the whole of it, either. Even in summer I rarely get farther than the terrace. It used to be very beautiful. Do you like what you have seen of it?"

"It's OK."

"But badly overgrown now, perhaps . . . Is it badly overgrown?"

"Not really. The front's all right. It's only round the side that—"

James bit his tongue. He felt a sudden rush of anger, as if he'd been tricked into saying too much, into confessing that he'd been round there exploring. The old man's voice went on without a hint of having noticed.

"I'm pleased. You must enjoy it while the weather does it justice. Well, I shall leave you to it and get back to my study. If there is anything you want, you have only to—"

"There is, actually. I want to know why this door's locked."

"I'm sorry?"

"This door. Behind the curtain. What's it for?"

"Door? Oh, it's not for anything. It's not a door, James."

"What?"

"It's not a door."

James didn't answer. He looked away, biting down his anger. But he knew the rules of the game by now. Lies were the privilege of adults. He shrugged.

"Well, James, enjoy the weather while it lasts."

"Thanks."

The old man scuffed away.

The dining room was empty. James went inside. Along the end wall by the garden he counted out the paces, toe to heel. Sixteen, seventeen, eighteen. In the corridor, another four to reach the curtain. Twenty-two feet between the corner of the house and the locked doorway.

He went outside, heading round the back towards the disused garden. From the corner of the house he counted out again as best as he was able, clambering his way across the rubble and the nettles. Twenty-two, as near as made no difference. He'd find out what the door looked like from this side. He scrabbled at the thickly matted stems.

The creepers slowly yielded, and showed what they'd been hiding.

Not a door, James.

James frowned. It made less sense than ever. The old man had been right, then. There wasn't any door here. Just a bricked-up square of nothing, and a cloud of long-dead dust.

11

James awoke. Night again, and darkness, and the same song calling. Waiting for his answer. He listened, frozen to his pillow. Then he struggled from the bedclothes, and pulled the curtains back.

He saw him.

The boy was standing just outside, below the terrace, in the single shaft of light from the old man's bedroom window. A tangle of black hair and a tanned face grinning. The teeth showed white. He raised his arm and waved. Behind him, long across the gravel, his shadow arm waved too, then turned aside and pointed: to the disused garden, in the darkness on his right.

James stared down.

"I'm dreaming. Dreaming I'm awake. Or awake?"

The boy's hand beckoned. James raised his own in answer.

He left his room and felt his way along the walls and down the staircase, pausing at each telltale creaking of the boards. There was no sound of waking. The house was deeply silent.

He reached the lower hallway.

There was moonlight on the heavy velvet curtain, folds of

light and shadow. He sidled in behind it. He pressed the handle downward, and softly stepped on through.

Quietly, he closed the door behind him. He was in the drawing room. Moonlight on the gilt, and on the empty stare of mirrors. His own face staring back as he crept forward. It looked frightened. Frightened in the mirrors, in the glass of the French windows. He slipped into the garden. A shadow came towards him from the shadows of the trees.

"Ben."

"I thought you weren't ever coming."

"Ben, I can't. Not tonight."

"But I've waited."

"Father will be back soon."

"James, you promised."

"It's the baby. He's ill. Mother's taken him away and Father's gone down with them. But he won't be staying on there. He'll be back."

"It gives us time, maybe?"

"Ben, I can't. He'll find me. He may be back at any minute. I've got to go to bed."

"Tomorrow, then?"

"I daren't."

"Tomorrow?"

". . . Yes, tomorrow."

"I'll whistle. Blackbird-whistle."

"Yes."

"You'll come?"

"Yes."

"You promise?"

"Yes. Tomorrow."

James turned, and stole away.

◆ ◆ ◆ ◆

"Tomorrow . . ."

James heard his own voice speaking. He was standing by the curtain in the ground–floor hallway.

"I've got to go to bed now. Or he'll find me."

He stared around him.

"I'm asleep."

He reached slowly forward, and pressed the handle downward. The door didn't move. *Not a door.* It was locked.

12

James awoke with the sunlight on his pillow. He clenched his eyes against it and turned over to avoid it. Then his head swung back. He looked towards the window. The curtains were wide open.

For an instant something stirred awake inside him, like a half-remembered shadow, the shadow of his dreaming. Then it slipped back into darkness, and was gone.

"Nosy Parker."

Who did she think she was, anyway? Coming into people's private rooms and drawing back their curtains while they were still asleep. He'd go and do the same to her tomorrow morning and see how *she* enjoyed it. He could have done without being awake at quarter past eight, too. It meant an extra hour to fill.

He reached the lower hallway and made his way along it to the kitchen. There was a smell of toast and coffee. Which must mean . . . The thought occurred too late, he was already in the doorway. His great-uncle was still in there, having breakfast.

Sarah smiled when she saw him.

"Oh, good morning, James. With the lark, is it?"

"What?"

"Up bright and early?"

"That's right. The sun woke me up."

"Well, that's what it's there for."

Ha. Ha. Bloody ha. James sat down with his great-uncle. The old man glanced towards him for a moment, then went back to his *Times*.

"Good morning, James."

"Morning."

"I trust you slept well?"

"Yes thanks."

"Good. Good. It's going to be a fine day again." He stated the fact as if he'd found it in the paper.

"Oh," James said. "Terrific."

He looked across. In spite of the sun, his great-uncle was still in the same old black suit and black waistcoat. Cold, James thought. Cold and skinny, everything about him, head, hands and heart. He felt himself shiver. The sort of old bloke whose skeleton had come to the surface, and was doing its best to get out.

"I see there's a letter for you this morning, James."

"What?"

His great-uncle had made the announcement as if, once again, he was reading it out of *The Times*. And, again, James felt oddly excluded. An afterthought, that's what it seemed like. News of no real importance. Like two days ago, in the study, the way he'd been told that his mother—

"A letter for you. It's on the table in the hall."

"There, James," Sarah said. "There's somebody who's got you in their thoughts, then."

He left the room quickly, not daring to let himself think why his heart had started to hammer. If he stopped himself thinking, he wouldn't be too disappointed—

But he was disappointed. The envelope was brown and officially printed, and his name and address had been typed. He shrugged, gouging it open and reading the eight or nine lines that were scribbled in pen. Then he crumpled it up and shoved it away in his jeans.

Sarah gave him his breakfast.

"Well?" she said. "Aren't you going to tell us what he says?"

"What who says?"

"Oh . . . well, the letter. I thought from the envelope it might be from that Mr. Dawes who brought you. But if—"

"Yes. That's right."

"Can you . . . can you tell us what he says?"

"Just that he hopes I'm having the time of my life and to write and let him know."

"Oh, I *am* pleased. You can write after breakfast, can't you? I've got a pad you can borrow—"

"And PS not to forget to report in to him at the end of this week."

"There, now. That was nice of him, wasn't it?"

"What was?"

"Well, thinking about you, and taking the trouble to write."

"It's his job."

"Yes, but I'm sure he wouldn't have if he didn't want to."

"He's got to keep tabs."

Sarah looked puzzled, as if she suspected a reference to cats. She didn't pursue it.

"Well, anyway," she said, "it's always nice to know that somebody's taking a bit of an interest, isn't it?"

She went back to her dishes. James ate in silence. The old man's eyes remained fixed on his paper. He crunched up his toast like dry bones.

With the pad on his knees at the foot of the oak tree, James chewed at his pen. He wrote.

> *Greville Lodge*
> *August 17th*
>
> *Dear Mr. Dawes,*
> *Thank you for your letter. I am very well. I watch telly and read a lot and do jobs for the housekeeper. The house is very interesting and the garden. I have still got a lot to discover. I won't forget to come this week to report. I have got the bus times from my great-uncle. He is very kind so there is no need for you to come and see me.*
>
> *Yours faithfully,*
> *J. E. Greville*

"That should keep the creep off my back for a bit, anyhow." He thought for a moment, then added a footnote.

> *P.S. I am sorry for what I did. I am sure what you said is right and staying here will help me reform.*

He grinned, and lit a cigarette.

The chunk of old brick smashed up into the ivy. It hit a thick stem and ricocheted off to the side. James's arm swung again. This time his missile did what he'd wanted: passed clean through the creepers and struck against what lay beyond. He lowered his sights, vertically downward, and repeated the process. After three more attempts he again made contact: the same sound of impact, a dull thud of brick against brick.

He wiped his hands on his jeans and went back to his place by the oak tree. Then he chewed at his thumbnail, his eyes gazing up at the house.

"Weird."

So that was that. If there were doors hidden away behind the cases of books on the two upper floors, they'd done a vanishing act by the time that they'd reached the outside. Bricked up, like the one down below. So why not the attic door, too, then? Perhaps it just hadn't seemed worth it, no one was likely to find it up there.

He hadn't got proof yet, of course, that there *were* two more doors, unless he was planning on shifting the book-shelves. Which might take a bit of explaining. And if there *weren't* two more doors, there could easily be some quite logical reason why they'd bricked up the one down below. Drafts, maybe. Or perhaps it just hadn't been needed: who'd need a door that led out into something that looked like an overgrown bomb site? But that still left the attic—a doorway that offered the cheerful surprise of a forty-foot drop into rubble and weeds.

Rubble.

He clambered to his feet and went back across. Burrow-ing about, he unearthed more chunks of old brickwork. Then he slowly stood up.

"Talk about *thick*."

He grinned. He'd seen it the first day he'd been here, from up in the cleft of the oak tree. *The shape of the house was all wrong. As if it just stopped dead when it reached this disused bit of the garden.* It was dead all right. Dead and gone. A whole section of it.

He went back to the oak and hoisted himself to the place where he'd had his best view of the house front. Yes, the front door and steps were off-center, too near this end by the derelict garden. But if you could picture another whole section . . .

He pictured it slowly, completing the wing of the house as it should be. So the corridors hadn't just stopped, they'd gone on through the doorways. But now they were nothing but ghosts going nowhere. Ghost corridors floating on into a part of the house that, somehow or other, had vanished away into air.

"But why? And when?"

He was going to find out. At least it would help fill the day up. But the question was how.

Old photos, perhaps. But even if they showed the part that was missing, they wouldn't show how it had vanished. He could ask his great-uncle. He dismissed the idea. He wasn't intending to ask any favors of *him*. Sarah, maybe? She'd told him she'd been here for most of her life, so she must have heard *something*. But, again, the idea of asking her questions—

"No way."

She'd start thinking he liked her. . . . He cursed obscenely. There was nobody else, so he'd just have to risk it. It was going to have to be her.

She was rolling pastry on the kitchen table. James slouched in the doorway, his hands in his pockets.

"Oh, hello, James. Too hot for you out there, is it?"

"Not really."

"Seventy-eight they say it's going to be. Too hot for pastry, really. Gooseberry pie today, it is—I hope that's all right?"

He didn't answer. He waited, then sidled on in, to a chair by the table, and sat there with one leg curled up beneath him, writing his name in the thin wraiths of flour.

"Written your letter, have you? To Mr. Dawes?"

"Yes, thanks."

"And you told him everything's all right, did you?"

"Yes."

"Oh good, I'm pleased. Well, it's nice to have a bit of company while I'm working, I must say. Not really one for the kitchen, your great-uncle, except for his breakfast. I'll take him his coffee through in a minute, I'm all behindhand this morning. So, what else have you been doing? Having a bit of a game in the garden?"

James bit back the answer he'd been going to give her. "That's right," he said. "Round in the part that's not used now."

"Not used?"

"Round the side. The weedy bit. Why's it not used now?"

"Oh well, you know how it is. Can't keep it all up, a place this size. Too big it is, really."

"It used to be bigger though, didn't it?"

"Bigger?"

"The house. It just looks as if it might've been, that's all. As if there might've been another part once, round the side."

The rolling pin moved faster.

"Oh, well . . . I dare say there was, once."

"How d'you mean: you dare say?"

"Well, I dare say, that's all. But that would've been a long time ago, I expect."

"What happened to it, then? This other part?"

"Now, how should I be expected to know?"

"I thought you said you'd nearly always been here. D'you mean you've never heard about it?"

"Well, I may have heard about it once, of course, but it's not important now, is it?"

"It's interesting, though. What happened to it?"

"Oh, that was a long time ago, I should think."

"What was?"

"Well . . . when it went."

"Why did it go?"

"Goodness, all these questions. Your great-uncle's the one for answering questions, not me."

"My great-uncle? Did it go in his time, then?"

"It might have, perhaps. You'd have to ask him. He wouldn't like it if—"

Her voice, and the rolling pin, stopped.

James turned round, following her eyes to the doorway. His great-uncle was there, looking in.

There was a moment of absolute silence.

"I'm sorry, Sarah. I was simply wondering about coffee."

"Oh . . . oh yes. I'm all behindhand. I . . . I was just chatting a bit to James."

"Yes. Well, don't let me interrupt you."

But he had. It was over.

James left the kitchen, clenching his fists in his pockets. He was going to find out, if it killed him. He paused at the foot of the staircase, glowering at the curtain. This house had gone on, once, on through these doorways, and he was going to discover—

His face changed expression. He frowned at the folds of the velvet.

He'd had a dream last night. Not a nightmare, a dream. A dream of . . . of what?

A thread of memory glimmered inside him, but when he tried to catch it, it faded out.

13

James struggled up and up through thick black sleep. He had to reach the surface. The song was up there, calling.

It was all right now. He was awake. He was sure he was awake. Like last time. But last time he hadn't been awake, only dreaming that he'd woken and dreaming that he'd gone down to the garden—

He'd do it now, again, he'd go down to the garden and then he'd know for certain. Out of bed now, and across the bedroom floorboards. He could feel them underneath him, bare feet, bare floorboards. But somewhere he could feel his head still on the pillow, dreaming he was waking, was walking

—I'm still in bed. But I'm awake. I *am* awake. In the morning I've got to know that I'm not dreaming. Remember. Remember in the morning. It's important. Yes. I'll write it down. If I write it down now, on the pad, I'll find it in the morning and I'll know. *Dear Mr. Dawes, I really am awake and the song is outside calling, so you needn't come and see me, I can't be dreaming.* And I can't be writing. My pen's in the wardrobe and I haven't got the pad now. It was Sarah's and it's downstairs in the kitchen. And if I'm not more quiet she'll wake up and then she'll hear me. So keep to the edge of the stairs. I'm awake now. Remember. Write it down now. Find the pen.

He felt for it, fumbling at the folds of the blankets. Found it, cold in his fingers, cold in the folds of the velvet blankets.

And slowly pressed it downward.

He stepped into the drawing room, and closed the door.

"Ben."

"You've come, then?"

"Like I promised."

"Your father?"

"He's asleep now."

"He won't find us?"

"No."

"Come on, then. Follow me."

August moonlight. The garden was carved in it, black and silver, as unreal as a summer frost. They passed across it, slow through the black, quick through the silver. Behind them the moon kept watch from the windows, and the face of the house was white.

"Where are we going, Ben?"

"Round through the orchard and up across the grove. Top-field then."

"Top-field?"

"That's where they are. You'll see."

James followed. The night was heavy with scents, apple and oak and elder, and where the grove ended, grasses and the darker scents of earth. Ben paused then.

"James, you wouldn't ever tell on me, would you?"

"Of course I wouldn't tell."

"Only—it's more than my life's worth, this is. Well, more than my post's worth, anyhow."

"Your post?"

"My job, here in the garden and that. I wouldn't want to lose it. Be the end of me, that would, be back where I started. And I'm not reckoning on going back there."

"I won't ever tell."

"All right, you just follow and I'll show you. Granny's footsteps, mind."

"What's that?"

"You walk where I walk, that's what it is. Follow in my footsteps, like. Or you won't have a foot left to go home with."

"How . . . how do you mean?"

"Have your foot off as soon as look at you, these things would. Come on, first one's over by the bank there."

They found it, hidden by a tussock of dandelion and rye-grass. Ben knelt down, drawing James beside him, and eased the leaves apart to show the gaping iron jaws.

"Well, there he is, ugly little blighter. And seven more like him, too, up across the field."

"I . . . I never thought they'd look so cruel, Ben."

"Oh, cruel all right, spring-traps are. That's what brings me."

"Do you come every night?"

"Course. No good missing, is it?"

"How do you put them out of action?"

"Spring them? Oh, that's easy enough, springing these old things. Do the lot in five minutes, I can."

"How do you know where they all are?"

"Because I help to set them, don't I? Me and old Durbon, we always set them ready, come evening."

"But why do you, if it's so cruel?"

"Orders, isn't it? Your father. Old Durbon takes orders from your father, and I take orders from old Durbon. Got to do what we're told, like."

"So what's different about the nighttime?"

Ben grinned. "My own free time, nighttime is. Do what I like then."

"You . . . you don't think any animals have been caught yet, do you?"

"Hope not."

"What animals are they meant for, Ben?"

"Foxes, that's what they're for really. Fox traps."

"Foxes? Are there foxes up here, then?"

"You needn't fret, they wouldn't hurt us. Wouldn't say boo to a goose, foxes. Well, maybe to a goose they would, not to us though."

"But if the foxes aren't stopped, they'll kill other things, won't they?"

"That's their affair, I reckon—in their natures, like. My nature's different, that's all. And, anyhow, there's stopping and stopping, that's what I say. Not right, these traps aren't, not human. And they don't pick and choose, either—snap up anything, they will, not just foxes. Badgers, squirrels, hedgehogs, anything. Can't be right, that. You'll get what I mean when we spring them, better than talking. You want to have a go?"

"All right."

"Stand up, then, and catch hold of this stick. Now you just picture you're an old badger, like, out for a bit of a stroll of an evening. That stick's your front leg. You just go ahead and touch it down on the spring-plate there. Only gentle, that's all that's needed."

James held his breath and edged the stick towards the foot-plate. The iron jaws snapped shut before he knew he'd touched it. He felt the impact in his stomach, like a gash of cold pain.

Ben looked up at him. "No good you letting go," he said. "Badger can't do that. You just catch hold again and try and get it free. There, see? No shifting that. Right through to the bone, that is. Only two options left now.

Wait here till you're done for good and proper. Or just go ahead and chew off that old leg of yours."

"They . . . they don't do that, do they?"

"Course they do, sometimes. Do anything to get back to a bit of freedom they will, poor beggars. No, not right it isn't, that's what I say."

"Hadn't we . . . hadn't we better go and spring the others, Ben?"

Ben stood up. "There, that's the spirit. And you'll not tell on me, will you?"

"No."

They moved from trap to trap, then sat together in the shadows of the hawthorn. High above the grove the moon made a hole in the darkness and the light streamed through across the meadow, turning the grasses white as hair.

"Ben . . ." James spoke with lowered voice. But even his whisper seemed to fill the stillness. "Ben, what does Durbon say when he finds all the traps shut in the morning, and nothing in them?"

"Doesn't have a chance of saying. I always offer to come and do it for him, see? Real grateful he is for that."

"So you're not really doing anything wrong, then, are you? At night, I mean. Just doing your morning job a bit early."

"One way of looking at it, I suppose. I don't reckon your father would be seeing it that way, mind. Likes his traps set ready, does your father."

"He would. He's that sort. I hate him."

"That's daft talk."

"You don't know him."

"I know he's given me a post here. That's enough for me."

"He makes you work hard enough for it."

"I don't mind work, do I? Not this sort, gardening and

all. Best thing that's ever happened to me, coming here. It's only the traps I don't hold with."

"Ben, the animals don't really do that, do they? Chew their own legs off?"

"I told you. That's what being trapped does for you. Do anything, you would."

James heard a change in the voice beside him. He glanced across at the lowered face.

"Ben, was it . . . was it so terrible where you were? Before you came here?"

"Yes."

"Is that how it felt? Like the spring-trap, I mean?"

"I reckon."

"Is that why you do it, come up here at night and everything?"

"Partly that. For the animals too, mind. Partly for them, partly for me, that's how it is."

"Couldn't you ever go out, then, where you were before? In the Home?"

"Oh, we could go out all right. Only a backyard there was, though, for a bit of football now and then. No garden. That's why I kept trying to run away, maybe, to find a bit of garden. Couldn't ever do it, though—always got me back in the end, they did. Like the spring-trap."

"What was it like, this Home?"

"A place for orphans, that's what it was. But I'm out now, leg and all. I don't want to talk about it really."

James didn't answer. He listened for a moment. An owl had awoken and was mourning in the grove.

"I don't know how you can come up here on your own at night, Ben. Owls are so eerie."

"Course they're not. They're only talking, same as you and me. I sleep out here sometimes."

"You don't . . . but you've got a room in the stable-block."

"Don't like rooms. Had enough of them, where I was. Lovely up here it is, with just the sky."

"I don't think I'd fancy it. I'd start imagining things. I don't mean just foxes. I mean—you know, ghosts and everything."

"Ghosts? Only in your head, ghosts are, not out here."

"I . . . I get nightmares sometimes." James bit his lip. "Ben, you won't tell anyone I told you that, will you?"

"Why should I? Nothing to be 'shamed of, nightmares. You want to try sleeping out a bit, that's all. No one could get nightmares, not out here."

"I'm really glad you're happy here, Ben."

"I'm that all right. It's being out of that place as does it. Midge'll be out of it too, soon. She'll be here by tomorrow."

"Midge?"

"My little sister—I told you. Proper strange it'll be, having Midge here. Proper strange for her too, what with her never knowing anything but the Home. Good, though. Good for both of us, being together."

"She's always been there, then, has she?"

"As near as makes no difference. Six years it'll be now, and she's only eight. Not one for gardens though, Midge. More for houses. It'll be a real treat for her, working in the kitchens, and Clara's going to see to her all right. She's a good sort, Clara is, always slips me a bit extra in my dinner-bag. Yes, Midge'll be all right. Always fancied herself as a lady, she has, in a big house. Like a pig in muck she'll be here."

"Sorry?"

"Duck to water. Take to it, like."

"I look forward to meeting her."

"Take to you, too."

"Will she?"

"Course she will. *I* have, haven't I? Seems funny really, me and you getting on."

"Why does it?"

"Well, what with you being up at the house and everything, and me only in the garden. I hardly even think about it now, though, and it's only been three weeks."

"I'm glad."

"You talk funny, mind. I still notice that."

"I don't, do I?"

"Well, it's one of us as does. And I don't reckon it's me. Any road, we'd better be making tracks soon. I've got to be up in the morning."

"Yes, I suppose so. I don't want to go, really."

"There's always tomorrow. Dinnertime maybe, down by the copse. Or I can whistle you up again if you like, tomorrow night."

"Yes. Yes, I'd like that. Only . . ."

"Only what?"

"Only you've got to be careful, Ben. If Father found out . . . well, I know him, that's all. He'd cut up nasty."

"Cut *me* up nasty, you mean? Cut my little paws off, like his spring-traps?"

"Don't say that."

"I was only joking."

"Well, don't say it."

"What's up, James?"

"Nothing . . . Oh, it's stupid, really. It just reminded me, that's all."

"What of?"

"Just a poem. It's a book I've had for ages. There's a poem in it that I never used to like, which only meant I used to read it more than all the rest."

"What was it?"

"It's only nursery stuff, really. It's about a boy called Little Suck-a-Thumb who . . . who gets his thumbs cut off by the scissor-man."

"But that's horrible."

"If you think that's horrible, you should see the picture that goes with it. It looks just like him. Like Father."

"No wonder you get nightmares."

"I know. Shall we go now, Ben?"

"No more we can do up here, any road. No trapping tonight, there won't be, and no maiming, so you can stop fretting, can't you?"

"Yes. But . . . but you will be careful, won't you?"

"Course I will. Come on."

14

The afternoon was a blaze of sunlight. The garden was baking, trapped in a blue dome of sky like a hot metal basin. James made his way through it, moving from shadow to shadow and cursing the flies that were after his blood.

He'd slept late, but he still felt exhausted. His head was muzzy and thick as if dreams had walked all night long through his sleep and not left him alone until daybreak, too tired to remember what they'd all been about.

He swatted his cheek, and moved on.

A gap in the high screen of bushes which ran the whole length of the derelict garden brought him out to an overgrown pathway. This must still be the grounds of the Lodge, then, bigger by far than he'd ever imagined. He ducked his way down through the tunnel of stems.

At the end, on his left, lay a tumbled confusion of timbers and brickwork. Outbuildings once. Stables, perhaps, from the old days. A few slabs of wall had survived and were still standing upright, but they rocked when he touched them. One shove of his foot sent them toppling down into dust.

Then an orchard, a hedged-in tangle of fruit trees knee-deep in grasses. The apples looked sick and neglected, half pulpy already, and specked with white pimples of mold. He left them untouched and came out again into sunlight. The thirsty dry whine of mosquitoes drove him aside to a grove of oak.

The air seemed heavier still here, thick and sour with

elder. *Apple and oak and elder . . .* He paused and looked around, frowning, as if the smell of the leaves had clicked open something inside him. Then he shrugged and went on.

The grove ended in a six-foot-high barrier of creosote fencing.

Again James paused, as if the sight of it vaguely surprised him. Two voices, one male and one female, came from beyond it. He hoisted himself to the top.

A sprawling new house, with a manicured lawn and a raked gravel driveway. A middle-aged man was plugging a mower to an extension cord draped through a window. In the center of the lawn was a blue plastic fish pond; a woman in pink rubber gloves was cleaning its edge with a bright blue rag. It was the woman who saw him first.

She mouthed discreetly across to her husband. The man glanced at James and stood up.

"What are you doing up there?" he said.

"Just looking, thanks."

"Do you make a habit of it?"

"Of what?"

"Of looking into other people's gardens."

"I didn't know it *was* a garden, did I, till I looked?"

"What were you expecting? A fairground?"

"No. A meadow." James spoke the words without thinking. He wondered why he'd said them.

"Are you trying to be funny?"

"Not specially."

"Well, you're not specially succeeding. In case you hadn't noticed, this is private property. And that includes the fence."

"Pardon me for contaminating it."

"Now look here—"

"How was I supposed to know it was yours, anyway? I thought it was my great-uncle's, didn't I?"

"Your . . . oh, I see. You're from the Lodge, then, are you? I didn't realize. But I'm afraid it still doesn't alter the fact that this is private property."

"So it's not part of Greville Lodge?"

"Not any more, no. Greville Lodge ends on the other side of that fence."

"But it used to be part of the Lodge, did it?"

"Used to, yes. Now, if you're sure you've got that point quite clear, perhaps you would be kind enough to—"

James didn't wait any longer. He heaved himself down and went back to the edge of the grove. He felt disappointed and angry. He didn't know why.

After a moment the mower began to purr like a razor, prim and proper and private. James pulled out his dart and volleyed it into the fencing. The mower clicked off into silence. Retrieving the dart, he belted away through the trees.

In the middle of the grove he stopped and listened. There was no sound of pursuit.

"Flaming Sloanes. What've they got to come here for, anyway, building all over other people's land?" He kicked idly at the stems of the elder. "Oh, what the hell. Makes no odds to me, anyhow."

But it did make odds to him, somehow. As if something he'd been expecting was missing. Deep inside him, he felt his angry disappointment grow.

A pinprick of pain in the crook of his arm brought his mind back to the grove. The blotches of sunlight were twanging with insects. He scratched at his elbow. A little raw lump, hot and cold like nettles, showed him that something had already bitten. He set off again, not back to the orchard but down through the part of the grove he hadn't explored yet, moving farther away from the house.

The oak trees and elders thinned and ended, giving way to a new blaze of sunlight. He stopped and looked out, shielding his eyes from the glare. For a moment he wondered what it was he was seeing. For a quarter of a mile on this side of the grove the land stretched away like a sheet of white metal, shimmering with heat haze, its surface as flat and unbroken as if it had melted. Close by his feet, it suddenly bubbled and blistered. Then it burst, and gave birth to a frog. James stood stock-still. It wasn't land he was seeing, it was water. He'd come out by the edge of a lake.

He took a step forward. The frog flipped away into safety. The circle of ripples grew broader and broader, and finally vanished far out near an uncertain shape in the heat haze which might perhaps be a small island. Was all this a part of Greville Lodge, too?

He followed the shoreline, keeping close to the side of the grove, swatting his way through the clouds of mosquitoes. They were worse now. The place was infested. The air smelt putrid, like drains.

The grove gave way to a tangle of nettles and brambles. Beyond them, up to his right, he could just catch a glimpse of tall chimneys and the ivy-grown tip of a gable. He was crossing the end of the derelict part of the garden.

He paused, dizzy with sunlight. His hair was glued thick to his forehead, his T-shirt and jeans were clinging with sweat. He grabbed at a low wooden post to stop himself falling, and looked down to see what it was.

It was one of a pair of rough uprights driven down into the water and attached to a small square of planking. Perhaps a landing-stage once. But the wood when he touched it felt rotten and spongy. No one had used it for years. From where he was standing he could already see the old beech copse, a few hundred feet farther on up the lakeside. If he cut up through there, he'd arrive on the lawn leading up to the terrace. Another five minutes would bring him back out where he'd started. Back to the house.

Back where he'd started. Back to Sarah, and teatime. Back to bloody probation . . .

The anger inside him tightened into a knot. He cursed, scratching at two new tingling lumps on his forearm. His fingernail drew blood.

Back to the house . . . or stay on down here and get eaten alive by mosquitoes, down by this stinking great bog-hole of water.

His leg lashed out. His kick struck the post and dislodged it. He drove the sole of his sneaker down hard on the platform of planking. Two of the timbers gave way. He stamped again, smashing the rest of the platform down under the water. A swarm of mosquitoes rose up towards him. He ran to the edge of the copse.

His anger had gone now. He felt suddenly sick and exhausted. He threw himself down in the shade of the beeches and dragged off his sneaker, flinging it from him to dry in the sunlight. Its whiteness was coated with sour green scum.

♦   ♦   ♦   ♦

James waited. It couldn't be long now. Until then he was safe here, hidden by beeches. He'd been very careful. No one had seen him come.

He watched the flicker of fish in the shallows, glass-clear, kaleidoscope-clear. Then he lifted his eyes to the flicker of sunlight on water, out to the tiny tree-covered island where white birds were wheeling. Someday, perhaps, he'd go out there, explore it. When his birthday came round, he'd ask for a boat.

He jumped and turned round as a hand touched his shoulder. Ben's face was smiling, close by his own.

"Sorry I'm late, James. I got put on the weeding. Takes ages, weeding does."

"That's all right."

"Then I had to go for my dinner-bag off Clara, and wait for her to rustle up some hazels. Always comes up with a few nuts, old Clara."

"Nuts? What for?"

"You'll see. And I've fetched along something else." He unstrapped his oilskin kitbag and fumbled about in the tools and twine. He handed a small battered book towards James. Its covers had long since gone. "For you, this is. A present."

"A present? Why?"

"Don't have to be a reason. Go on, take it."

"I can't take this, Ben."

"Course you can. I want you to."

James took it. It was *Robinson Crusoe*.

Ben sat down by a tree. He looked happy. "Best book ever written, that is. Well, only one I've ever read, really."

James sat down beside him and turned the thumbed pages. He didn't tell Ben that he had his own copy, bound in green leather. He'd once tried to read it, but found it too hard.

"Have you read all this, Ben?"

"Course. Leastways, all but the big words. Makes no odds though, leaving them out. Only for show, big words are. Story's still the same."

"What . . . what's it about?"

"Being shipwrecked and marooned, and starting up all on your own. Building up your own place out of nothing. My dream, that is, living like that. Sounds easy when you read it, mind, making cabins and things, but it's harder when you . . ."

He stopped suddenly, and lowered his eyes.

"Harder when you what?"

"James, you wouldn't tell on me, would you, if I told you?"

"You're always asking me that. Don't you trust me?"

"Course I do. Ought to by now, oughtn't I, with all you know? Spring-traps and such? I was reckoning on telling you sometime, anyhow. Sharing it, like."

"Can you tell me now?"

"In a bit. In a day or two, right?"

"All right."

"Biggest secret I've got, this is. Be the finish of me if it got out."

"It won't through me, anyway." Reluctantly James let the subject rest, and fingered the pages again. "Where did you get the book, Ben?"

"Only book in our house, that was. It was Dad's really— don't reckon he ever read it, though. Sunday School Prize, it was. Can't imagine our dad at Sunday School, somehow. Boozing Prize, more like."

"What happened to the covers?"

"Used 'em for lighting the fire, knowing him. Picture at the front there was once, too, but that's gone the same."

"It doesn't matter. Thanks, Ben."

"Make your own pictures, I reckon. Pictures in your head, like, they're the best ones." He rummaged again in the oilskin bag. "Have my dinner now, right? You want to share? It's cheese and pickles."

"No, you go ahead. We'll be eating up at the house in half an hour, anyway."

"Expect it's roast pheasant, is it?"

"I doubt it."

"I've heard all about your banquets all right."

"I'd rather have cheese and pickles any time."

"You're a dafter beggar than I reckoned, then. Don't know you're born, you don't. No more do I these days, come to that. Pig in muck here, I am, just like our Midge."

"She's settling in, then, is she?"

"Settled in already, and only been here a day. I knew she would."

"I still haven't seen her."

"Only seen her a couple of times myself, what with her being in the kitchens. You'll meet her all right, though. Tomorrow maybe, up the orchard, if I can fix it with Clara."

"I'd like that. As long as . . . as long as Father doesn't find out. He doesn't approve of . . ."

"Of mucking in with servants?" James didn't answer. "It's all right, anyhow, he won't find out, James. Clara won't let on. She's a good one, old Clara is, she's going to be a real mum to our Midge and no mistake."

He munched at his dinner, contented, and swigged ginger beer from a bottle. He handed the bottle across to James.

"Thanks. Ben, what happened to your own mother?"

"Died, Mum did, years back. Pneumonia, that was. And Dad not long after. Scaffolding it was with him."

"Scaffolding?"

"Fell off it, like."

"Oh."

"That's why we were stuck in that Home. Yours still away, is she? Your mum?"

"Yes, she's staying on down at the coast for a while. The sea air's supposed to be good for the baby. I only wish Father would go and join her."

"Got it in for him all right, haven't you?"

"I told you before—you don't know what he's like."

"Belt you, does he?"

"No, of course he doesn't belt me. I wish he would, sometimes. At least it would be *something*."

"That's daft, that is. Mine used to all right. Hurt like nobody's business."

"Father's got his own ways of hurting. That's why I'm scared he . . ."

"Hello, *hello*. Who've we got here, then?"

James turned his head. A yard away from the oilskin kitbag, sitting bolt upright, a gray squirrel watched him.

"Dinnertime, is it?" Ben clicked his tongue and scrabbled again in the kitbag. The squirrel flicked closer, poised again. Between his teeth, Ben cracked a hazel. "Beech, this is. Come for his nuts. Always hunts me down, old Beech does, come dinnertime."

James watched, transfixed, as the squirrel took nut after nut from Ben's fingers. "How did you tame him, Ben?"

"Don't need taming, squirrels. Just nuts. You want a go? You can give him the last one."

"I couldn't."

"Course you could."

"What do I do?"

"Nothing. He does the doing." Ben cracked the final nut and handed James the kernel.

The squirrel came at once, like a toy, a piece of living clockwork. Upright on its haunches, one paw on James's finger, it took the hazel from him. Its touch awoke something deep inside him, like laughter.

Then it was over. Beech was gone.

James was silent. A breeze came, bringing freshness and smells of cool water. He watched it shivering the surface of the lake.

"Do you know, Ben, I don't think I'd ever noticed them before."

"Noticed what?"

"The squirrels."

"Must be blind, then. Hundreds in the copse, there are, and up the grove. Have a rare old time of it in this place, they do, with the trees."

"That's not what I meant, really . . . How much more magic have you got up your sleeve, Ben?"

"What? Old Beech, you mean? No magic about old Beech."

"Not to you, maybe."

Ben glanced up from his bread and smiled. Then he went back to his munching, thoughtful for a while, looking out across the lake.

"See that little old island over there, James?" he said.

"Yes. Why?"

"Just wondering."

"I was only thinking about it earlier on, before you got here."

"That a fact? Ever been out there, have you?"

"No. Nobody goes out there."

"That a fact?"

"What's so funny? There's nothing on it but a few trees and ducks, I shouldn't think."

"That a fact?"

"Why do you keep on saying that? It *is* a fact, anyway. Nobody's ever set foot on it as far as I know."

"That's what old Robinson Crusoe thought. Till he found the footprint."

"Ben, what are you on about?"

"I just told you—footprints. You might go over to that old island—"

"I haven't got a boat, have I?"

"You might go over to that old island and find footprints, like."

"It's not very likely, is it? Whose footprints am I likely to find over there?"

"Never can tell. Might be Man Friday's." Ben's teeth flashed a white grin and sank into an apple. "Then again, might be mine."

15

James came to with a start. He'd been sleeping. Somewhere a voice was calling, in a long beckoning cry.

"*Hello-o-o . . . Where are you?*"

Where was he? He didn't know.

Then a stench of rank water told him. He turned his head slightly. Leaves crackled under his cheek. He blinked at the sick glare of sunlight.

"*Hello-o-o . . .*"

The voice came again, from the lawn up beyond the beech copse.

"*Where are you? . . . It's me.*"

It was her. It was teatime.

He stayed there, unmoving. In his ears was the whine of mosquitoes, and the whine of his own shrill blood. He felt wretched.

"*Hello-o-o . . .*"

He clenched up his eyes and buried his head in his arm.

♦ ♦ ♦ ♦

"*Hello-o-o . . . Where are you? . . . It's me.*"

The voice came from the lawn, on the other side of the stables. Ben leapt up from the grass in the orchard and looked down at James with delight.

"It's her!" he said. "It's Midge! I knew she'd come!"

"Does she know where we are?"

"I told her the orchard. Don't know what an orchard is,

though, old Midge, like as not. You wait on here and I'll go and fetch her along before she goes hollering the whole place down." He stuck his finger and thumb in his mouth and whistled. The calling immediately stopped.

Ben ran off to the tunnel of trees which led from the orchard out to the garden. Then he suddenly turned and ran back.

"James, there is one thing."

"What's that?"

"You'll have to be 'Master James' while she's around."

"I will not."

"You will that. She'll start calling you 'James' in company, else. When your father's about. Can't be expected to keep chopping and changing, can she? And she wouldn't understand why she had to, anyhow. She's only eight. So it's 'Master James,' right?"

"Well, *she* can, then. But I'm not having *you* doing it."

A floundering of bushes made them both turn. Midge broke through into sunlight. She stood with her hands on the hips of her little black dress.

"Ben!" she said crossly. "*Here* you are. You were *hidin'*."

"Course I wasn't. Daft."

"You *were*. And I only got five minutes."

James looked across at her, startled. He was seeing an eight-year-old Ben. A miniature Ben, with one front tooth missing, paler and thinner than the Ben who was racing towards her. But a few years of sun and of growing would bring out her beauty. The dark hair and eyes were already like his.

He watched as Ben hugged her and lifted her, swinging her round until she was screaming with laughter. And he felt the same laughter inside him, and a sudden odd shadow of loneliness too.

"Ben, you stop it! You'll go and mess me all up!"

Ben swooped her back onto her feet and held her at arm's length, his hands on her shoulders, looking. She smoothed herself down, indignant again.

"What they done to your hair, Midge?"

"Curled it. With papers. Clara done it." She patted it proudly, then looked slightly doubtful. "Looks daft, don't it?"

"Course it doesn't look daft. Real treat, it is. And a new dress too. Proper lady you are already, Midge, and no mistake."

"Got me own bed now, too. In Clara's room."

"Blimey, you won't be talking to me soon, gardener's boy."

"No, I won't that." For a few seconds she held the look of prim indignation, then she threw herself forward and buried herself in his arms. "Yes, I will. Course I will. Daft."

"Now then, Midge." Ben disengaged her. Flushed with pleasure, he turned towards James. "Us going on like this, and somebody waiting to say hello. This is Master James, Midge."

"Oh . . ." She looked up at James as if she had only just seen him. Then she bobbed a small curtsy.

James felt himself blushing. "Hello, Midge. I . . . I can call you Midge, can I?"

"You can if you like. It's not my *real* name, but I don't mind. It's what Ben calls me. 'Cause I'm little."

Ben grinned. "'Cause you're a pest, more like."

She gave him a withering look, then curtsied again to James.

James's blush deepened. "You . . . you don't have to curtsy, Midge."

"I do."

"Really you don't. Not with me."

"I do, then. I been *told*. By Clara."

"Well, I'm telling you now, Midge."

Midge looked confused, then a bit disappointed.

"I like doin' it," she said. "I been practicin'. And I can't help meself doin' it now I've started. Me leg goes without me."

She bobbed again as if to confirm it, then drew herself loftily up.

"I come here in a *car*," she said. "And I been makin' *jam*."

"Oh . . . really?"

"And I'm going to be a parlormaid one day."

"Are you? That's . . . that's wonderful. I like your new dress, Midge, it really suits you."

"Yes." She smoothed it again, then suddenly lifted it up to her chin. "I got new bloomers, too," she said.

James looked away. All Midge's dignity left her. She reddened and hunched up her shoulders, giggling into her hand.

"Now, Midge," Ben said. "That's no way to be going on in front of Master James."

"Well, they *are* new," she said. "Clara gave them to me. I got to get back to her now, too, or she'll be wonderin'."

"She won't mind, not for another minute or two."

"She will that. I got to help with a pie."

"I'll come up and see you later on then, shall I, up the kitchen? Teatime maybe?"

"All right. I may be busy, mind. Or I may be *hidin'*." She looked arch for a moment, then reached her hand forward, slipping it into his own. "No, I won't be. I'll be waitin'."

They went with her, as far as the end of the tunneled pathway, and watched her skip off to the kitchen. By the time she'd reached it she'd bobbed two more curtsies, to sparrows she'd met on the lawn.

Ben shook his head. "She's a caution, old Midge is. It's good having her here. I've never seen her more proud—thinks every day's a Saturday now, she does. You do like her, James, don't you?"

"Who wouldn't?"

"She's got a real shiner on you and all."

"How do you know that?"

"Oh, I know all right. Sees herself as Lady James Greville already."

"Come off it, Ben."

"Always dreamed about being a lady, old Midge has, I told you. Some lady she'd make, though, picking her nose."

"I didn't really know what to say to her."

"You don't have to, with Midge. She does the saying. Anyhow, James, I'm grateful."

"Grateful?"

"To your father, for having her here. For getting her out of the Home."

"There's no need. It's not charity. She'll have to work for it, the same as you do—he'll make sure of that. And he'll probably never even set eyes on her."

"No matter. Long as she's happy. Don't go looking like that, then. It'll stick like it."

"What?"

"Your face. Stick like it, it will, if the wind changes—frowning all over."

"Sorry."

"That's all right." Ben was thoughtful for a moment, chewing a stem. Then he looked up and grinned. "Tell you what. Got something to show you. To cheer you up, like."

James felt a sudden thrill of excitement. "Something . . . something to do with what you were saying yesterday?"

"That's right. Like I promised. Good a time as any, I reckon."

Ben led him, back through the orchard and down through the grove, then round to the left up the shore of the lake. He stopped where the rushes grew thickest.

"Best hidden bit of the lake, this is," he said. "Can't see it from up the grounds, not from any direction. Specially nighttime."

"Nighttime?"

Ben didn't answer. He bent down. Lifting a matting of reeds and dry branches, he slowly uncovered a sheet of tarpaulin.

"Here it is, then. Homemade, mind, so not much to look at. But it serves."

He slid the tarpaulin aside.

James looked, hardly breathing. A platform of logs and old timbers, corded together. A raft.

◆ ◆ ◆ ◆

"Hello-o-o . . . James, where are you?"

James jolted upright. His head was still pounding. He didn't want to wake up.

He'd been dreaming, he thought, dreaming a dream that he'd like to go back to. Of voices calling . . .

The voice called again. Nearer. Half-drugged with sleep, he forced himself out into the brilliant sunlight to pick up his sneaker. It was almost dry.

"Are you there, James?"

He'd have to go now, or she might come down here and find out about . . . about what? There was something down here by the lake that she mustn't discover, something hidden. . . . He shook his head sharply and dragged on his shoe.

"Barmy."

Dreaming, that's all. Later, he'd try and remember. He tore away, up through the trees.

Sarah was on the lawn, looking.

"Oh, James, there you are. It's teatime. I thought I'd lost you—I've been calling for three or four minutes."

"I hadn't run away, if that's what you mean."

"No, of course that's not what . . . James, you look so *hot*."

He ducked his forehead away from the palm of her hand. "I'm OK. Just got a bit of a headache, that's all."

"Well, come on back to the kitchen. It's far too hot to be walking around out here, and you with no hat on. You must've been miles, the time you've been."

"Not really. Only up through those oak trees. I couldn't get any further anyway, could I, with that fencing in the way? Who's been building there?"

"The Smythes, you mean? Oh, they're ever so nice. They bought the field off your great-uncle a year or so back. It's a little bungalow like that that *we* could do with, really. Not this great big place."

"I don't see why."

"It's so hard to keep it all up and . . . James, what's happened to your poor arm?"

"Only a couple of bites or something from down by the water. I'll probably survive."

"You've been scratching them."

"They were itching, weren't they?"

"Well, we'll get some ointment on them. You shouldn't have gone down by the lake, really, this weather. It's not nice, with all those insects."

"I didn't know there *was* a lake till I got there, did I?"

"So bad it's got, these past few years, a proper eyesore. If I had my way, it'd all be filled in."

"No!" The protest in his voice surprised even James. He felt Sarah's eyes on him. She'd been right, anyway, the lake was a filthy great eyesore. He wondered what had made him defend it.

"Well, you needn't worry, I'm sure," she said. "I shouldn't think it'll be filled in while your great-uncle's alive. Not one for too many changes, Mr. Greville's not. He might think different, mind, if he ever got down there and saw the state of it. Still, he'll be pleased to hear you like it."

"I never said I did, did I?"

"But I thought you just said—"

"I'm going to have a lie down after tea, if that's all right."

"Yes . . . yes, of course. Oh dear, I hope it's not a bit of sunstroke."

So did he. If it was, he'd never be shot of her fussing about. She'd have a flaming great field day.

He followed her up the steps from the lawn and along the terrace. Through the window of the study he caught a glimpse of his great-uncle resting, laid out on the couch like a corpse.

Some hope.

Sarah stopped by the door to the kitchen. "Perhaps you'd better slip those shoes off," she said. "They look in a bit of a mess."

"It's only one of them. It got in the water, that's all."

"How did you go and do that?"

"There was a platform-thing. My . . . my foot sort of went through it."

"Oh, that was the old landing-stage, I expect. Not that there were ever any boats here to my knowledge, your great-uncle didn't hold with them. There—you take the other one off as well and we'll give them a bit of a cleanup in the morning. A pity, I always used to think, not having a boat. I often used to think it would've been nice to go and float out there and have a look round. There's a bit of an island in the middle."

"I saw."

"Nothing on it though, I shouldn't imagine, but a few

trees and ducks. Nobody's ever set foot there as far as I know."

"What . . . what did you say?"

"I said nobody's ever set foot . . . James, are you *sure* you're all right? You're looking ever so flushed."

James didn't answer. He wanted to sleep, he was weary. As if his head were clogged with thick scum, thick darkness. And as if all the time, something was trying to break through, to break surface, and float out freely. Float out into the light.

16

The bed was floating. Or James was, suspended six inches above it, floating in darkness, too dizzy and too light-headed to sleep.

His eyes wouldn't close, his eyelids felt full of hot sawdust. And their burning had spread to his face and his forearms. The sheet was like sandpaper, rubbing them raw.

His mouth was parched dry. He pulled himself upright and fumbled about for his mug of cold water. It was already empty.

The hands of his watch showed a quarter to two.

He got up and looked out. There was no breath of movement. The night was heavy and sour, with a cheesy moon in the beech copse. Down below, on the lawn and the terrace, his great-uncle's window shone yellow. So his light was still on even now, at a quarter to two in the morning. Perhaps the old scarecrow was scared of the dark.

"Listen who's talking." James stopped on his way to the bathroom. "Enough to scare the hell out of anybody, this place."

The passage was empty of all but the moonlight. But somewhere the boards were still creaking, like the tread of old footsteps, old ghosts that couldn't find rest. He hurried on into the bathroom and turned on the tap to a trickle. Even the trickle made the pipes judder, enough to awaken the dead. Or worse, to awaken Sarah. She'd hear him, come up and find him, start rabbiting on about sunstroke and nightmares. He cursed her, and turned the tap off.

Milk, then. In the fridge in the kitchen. If he was careful and kept to the edge of the staircase . . .

He reached the ground floor undetected and crept along into the kitchen. In the fridge he found what he needed. He guzzled it straight from the carton, thrilling at its ice-cold spill down his chin and his chest.

Then he stood undecided. He felt restless. Unsatisfied, somehow, in spite of the milk. Like an emptiness deep down inside him, a vague sense of something he longed to go back to. London, maybe. It had been all right, London. Risky as hell, but all right. But the thought of his friends didn't seem to appeal now. The thing that he wanted was nearer than London. Something up here at the Lodge . . . ?

He snorted. If *that's* what he reckoned, he *must* have got sunstroke. He crumpled up the carton and kicked it away out of sight.

Just past two. He ought to get up to his bedroom. The idea of it started him sweating. He pressed his bare back to the fridge. It was hotter upstairs—at least the kitchen had flagstones, not carpets. He could stay for a while. He could do just whatever he wanted. If he wanted more air, he could even . . . His eyes went across to the door which led out to the garden. On the mat where he'd left them at teatime, his sneakers showed pale in the moonlight. Side by side, with the heels towards him, as if they were waiting. He slipped them on quickly and eased back the bolts on the door.

It was lighter out here than he'd banked on, and even more silent. He kept to the grass, avoiding the telltale gravel. Slithering down the slope from the terrace, he moved away over the lawn.

He threw himself down on the bench at the edge of the beech copse. He was safe here, in shadow, with a view of the house front. He looked across.

There was no sign that Sarah had heard him, her room was in darkness. But his great-uncle's light was still burning. He wasn't in bed yet. James could just see him, in his chair by the open window, his head slightly forward. Reading maybe, or asleep.

In spite of himself, he felt glad of the old man's presence. It was strange being out all alone in the dead hours of darkness. If he *was* all alone. . . . There were animals, Sarah had told him. Badgers and hedgehogs. And foxes. He drew up his legs on the bench seat. If it wasn't so hot, he'd go in. But even out here it was stifling. The air was unfresh, as if someone had already used it. Leftover air from the daytime, full of stale sunlight. The memory of sunlight made him feel dizzy and sick.

He wouldn't stay long. Just as long as the light was still on in the window. The minute it vanished, he'd get up and go.

He waited and watched. His head was beginning to spin now. The bench started lurching. He clung to it tightly and clenched up his eyes.

Then only blackness and sounds of the nighttime. The sound of the barn owls spooking the grove. A fidget of movement from down in the rushes. The squawk of a duck, and a flurry of feathers. A splashing of water, away on the lake.

◆ ◆ ◆ ◆

The raft came free of its mooring. With his trousers rolled

up above knee-height, Ben splashed through the shallows and clambered aboard it. It lurched and then steadied, and started to float.

"You shift back a bit, James, and I'll go in front. Then we'll try the paddles." The raft lurched again. Ben's whisper was full of laughter. "And you'd best stay kneeling if you don't want a wet bum."

"I've got one already."

"Sorry about that. Bit low in the water, she is, not being used to two. Drier to swim it, I reckon. Quicker, too."

"No thanks. You haven't ever swum it, have you?"

"Once or twice I have. Before I built her, that was. Come on, let's give the paddles a go."

"How did you make them, Ben?"

"Bits of old fencing. You dip when I do—you left side, me right."

The blades shoveled the water, scoopfuls of moonlight, mercury-bright.

"How do you manage this on your own, Ben?"

"Not much better than we're managing with the two of us. Zigzag, like. We'd best try more rhythm, or we'll still be tacking about come daybreak."

They floundered on lamely, stifling their laughter, at odds with each other. Then they found what they wanted, moving together, the one rhythm, of bodies and arms and water. James felt it thrill through him, like a thrill of danger. They were out in the open, completely exposed.

"Are you sure we're out of sight from the garden, Ben? And from the house?"

"Should be. I'm not turning round to find out, though. No looking back, that's what I say. Best motto."

"Yes."

"Shouldn't be in line with the house till we're on the

island, my reckoning. We'll be safe round the back of her then, though, with the pine trees between."

"Where do we land?"

"Left-hand side of her, up in the rushes. Wake the ducks."

"Are there many?"

"Plenty of mallards. Moorhens, too. Won't mind though, being woken. Know my ways by now."

"How often do you come here?"

"Most nights. Work to be done, like."

"Work?"

"You'll see. You just keep paddling, she's never gone this easy. Got a way with you, you have."

"You wouldn't say that if you could see me. I'm drenched."

"Soon be there now."

James leant slightly forward. The island rose up through the curve of Ben's neckline and shoulder, half screened by his tangle of hair.

In another two minutes the paddles struck bottom.

"OK, James. Might as well get a bit wetter now we've started. Quicker to pull her in from here."

The raft beached softly. James looked around him. Pine trees, long bars of moonlight and shadow. The stirring of reed beds. The waking of ducks.

"She'll be all right, James, no tide to take her. You follow me. It's up here, round the back."

Ben's cabin was hidden. Three walls of old timber, corded to pine trunks. A roof of tarpaulin, nailed across them. The fourth side wide open to let in the night.

"You built this, Ben?"

"It didn't grow."

"But when?"

"Nighttime. My free time."

"It's amazing."

"Ducks think so too—been in again by the looks of it, leaving their messages. All right by me, though, so long as they don't go blabbing to old Durbon."

"Are you going to build the last wall?"

"I don't reckon. Feel less closed in, like. My own place this is, built to suit. Never had that before. James, it's . . . it's not wrong, is it?"

"Wrong?"

"I've taken nothing that's wanted, only old timber, stuff chucked away. And the cording was saved for out of my wages."

"Of course it's not wrong."

"It's not my land, though. I'm here without asking."

"Nobody uses it. Nobody ever comes here, you said so yourself. It's yours now. Settlers' rights."

"Yes."

"So it's all right. It's more than all right. And no one's ever going to find out, anyway. Have you told Midge?"

"Too young yet. She'd talk. Only you."

"What are you planning on doing here next?"

"I'll try and make chairs later, somewhere for sitting. And I'll sleep here come next summer, maybe."

"I've got chairs you can have, Ben. And a blanket and a pillow. We can bring them across on the raft."

"No, stealing that'd be, from the house. Only my own stuff this has got to be. That's all part of it. Other stuff'll bring trouble. I've got no right to it."

"But it'll be *my* stuff, from my bedroom. I've got masses more than I need. Mrs. Rogers won't notice, I'm sure she won't. And even if she does, it won't matter."

"No, I couldn't do that."

"You've got to, Ben. I want you to have it. As . . . as a present. Tomorrow, all right?"

"I'll consider. Not that I'm not grateful, mind. It's just that . . . well, I'll consider. Come on, I'll show you the rest of the place now we're here. There's only a few yards of it."

They followed it round, emerging again on the house side, and looked out across at the dark clumps of beech copse and grove where the owls were already waking. Then James touched Ben's arm and drew back.

"What's that light, Ben?"

"Where?"

"Over there. Up between the copse and the grove. It's in the house, isn't it?"

"Could be, I suppose."

"There's nowhere else it could be. Can you see which room it's in?"

"Course I can't, with the trees. And I wouldn't know even in daylight, not up the house."

"It . . . it looks as if it might be in my room, that's all."

"You didn't leave it on, did you?"

"No."

"Well, that's all right then, isn't it? It's your father's room, maybe."

"But it's way past midnight."

"Gone to the bathroom, like as not."

"Yes . . . yes, like as not."

Ben put his arm round his shoulder and grinned reassurance.

"There, picking up the lingo, you are. Soon have you talking right, we will."

"What?"

" 'Like as not.' Must be the company you're keeping."

James was glad of the arm. He felt cold now. They stood for a moment, not speaking, looking across at the shore.

"Wishing-well," Ben said.

"Sorry?"

"Wishing-well. The lake. Look at her."

The lake was pure silver. The moon lay inside it, sky-deep, like a coin.

"Have whatever you want, you can now, James, so long as you believe hard enough. Best time this is, for wishing, with the moon in her."

James wished. But even as he wished, he knew that he didn't believe it. He watched the lake's surface, half expecting the sign which he dreaded. A cloud would cross it, a mallard would smash it apart.

"Never seen her this clear I haven't, James, not all the times I've been over."

No cloud came, and no mallard. But James knew that the lake was lying. What he had wished for couldn't last long now. Something would happen to end it.

He raised his eyes slowly. The light in the house had gone out.

◆　◆　◆　◆

James shivered. His shiver awoke him. The light in the house had gone out now, but a new light was rising beyond it, a thin skin of daylight. The night was dissolving to mist on the lawn.

His body was cramped from the bench seat, but the burning had left it. Stiffly, he pulled himself up.

"I must be cracked or something, sleeping out here."

Anything could have got him, badgers, foxes . . . werewolves, more than likely. She'd probably forgotten to mention those.

He rubbed at his shoulders.

Behind him, out on the lake, a bird splashed on water. He turned his head sharply and listened, not moving. The sound died away.

"It was a duck, that's all."

But he still made no movement, as if the sound held a meaning he couldn't be sure of. For a moment it had made him feel happy, then oddly uneasy.

He shivered again in the first cold of morning, and hurried away to his bed.

17

James stood at his bedroom door, listening. There was only the sound of the blood in his eardrums. The house was still silent. For the second time in ten minutes, he fumbled his way down the stairs.

The weight dragged at his shoulders but he didn't dare move any faster. He couldn't see where he was going, he'd knock something over. He'd be found out.

He paused on the landing and listened again. Then, tread by tread in the darkness, he bundled on downward. His bare feet met flagstones. He was in the hall.

At the foot of the staircase the drawing room door was ajar as he'd left it. He passed through quickly, across to the open French windows. A shadow met him, detaching itself from the trees.

"I've got them," James said. "Where's the first load gone to?"

"Down in the rushes."

"Already?"

"Thought it best, while I was waiting."

"Shall I come with you? Help you carry this lot?"

"No, you go back in. I'll manage. And . . . and thanks, James."

A hand squeezed his shoulder. The bundle was lifted from him. Ben's shadow, heavy with pillow and blankets, vanished again into night.

18

The frog writhed, like rubber.

James held it upside down on its back, its sides gripped hard between thumb and fingers. He wondered what he could do with it. Now it'd taken him half an hour to catch, he wasn't intending to waste it. He looked at the bloated belly. A pity he'd not got his dart.

He could take it up to the kitchen, drop it down on the table, tell Sarah he wanted it cooked for his supper. They did that stuff over in France. But, knowing her, she'd probably do it. Anything to give him something he fancied.

He could always shut it in the old cow's handbag and give her a Creepshow all of her own.

Wasted on her, though. He began to lose patience.

If he had a straw he could stick it right up its bum and blow till he burst it. He'd read about that.

His fingers tightened. The legs were floundering, longer and longer. He yanked at the flippers.

"Snip! snap! snip! They go so fast,
That both his thumbs are off at last."

He grinned and squeezed harder. Yellow slime squirted out on his wrist. With a yell he dropped it, and leapt too late to stop its escape through the rushes.

"Sod you!"

He picked up a branch and smashed it down into the water, then chucked it away and wiped at his wrist in disgust. Well, he wasn't going to waste *another* half hour this morning, but next time was going to be different. The next one he caught would go straight in her handbag. He wasn't missing his chances again.

For a minute or two he kicked about in the beech copse. He was restless again, more restless than ever, and exhausted after his night in the garden. This place was getting his back up. He wondered why he didn't just go.

Go where, though? Not London. They'd look there, and anyway London seemed to have lost its attraction. Liverpool, then? Or Sheffield? But wherever he went he was going to need money—a damn sight more than his one pound twenty-five pence.

And there was something else, too. Somewhere, right at the back of his mind, he still had a sense there was something round here that he wanted, or something he needed to finish. Something to do with that bit of the house that had gone now? He'd still got no further finding out about that. Or something to do with the dreams he'd been having but couldn't remember? He *had* to remember. But the effort of trying brought on his headache. He couldn't be bothered now. He slumped back against a tree.

He rested his eyes for a moment and let himself drift on the sounds of the morning. Buzzing and bird-song. A crunching of footsteps, up on the drive . . .

◆　◆　◆　◆

The sound made James turn. She was here on the drive right behind him, panting and bobbing.

"*Hello*, Midge. How are you?"

"I'm puffed. I been runnin'."

"Did you want me?"

"Mrs. Rogers told Clara and Clara told me to tell you, special."

"Tell me? Tell me what."

"Sir wants you."

"Father? Where is he?"

"Oh . . . she never said. D'you want me to go and ask and come back?"

"No, of course not. I'll find him."

"And . . ." Her sudden shy giggle showed the gap in her teeth. She covered it with her hand. "And I brought you this."

"This is for me, Midge?"

"If you want it."

"Of course I want it."

"I made it. First one I ever done."

"It's beautiful."

"No, it's not. The eyes've gone wonky."

"It's still beautiful."

"I got to go now."

Her footsteps receded. James stood where she'd left him, holding the little gingerbread man.

◆　◆　◆　◆

His head nodded down on his chest. He shook it, and listened. The footsteps had stopped now. There were voices up in the garden, a man's voice and Sarah's. Then, a few minutes later, the sound of a motor. He left the tree and went back through the copse.

On the pathway beyond it, he paused.

The motor mower was ancient, a filthy great thing like a First World War tank. And the man on it wasn't much younger, or cleaner. James stood and watched him shaving long strips from the lawn. Not very straight strips. He was a lousy driver. James found the fact cheering: the bloke might be worth checking out.

He moved a step forward, catching the old man's eye as the lawn mower rattled towards him and swung at the edge of the pathway. They nodded, not speaking or smiling. James watched the departing back.

His spirits rose higher. He knew the type well, he could pick out a slacker a mile off. And this was a slacker if ever he saw one. The bloke was all right.

When the lawn mower came to a halt by the pathway, he sauntered towards it.

"I'll do it," he said. He unhooked the grass box. "You the gardener?"

"Could say that."

"What's your name?"

"Who's asking?"

"James."

"What're you doing round here?"

"Been sent here. A bit of hassle back home in London. You know—ran out of luck."

The old man eyed him, then nodded. "Alf," he said.

"Where's this stuff dumped, Alf?"

"I'll show you."

Alf led him along the path and off through a gap in the rhododendrons. A tree had been felled here, leaving a few yards of clearing, with a small timbered shed and some coils of wire netting. James emptied the box at the side.

Alf had sat down already, on a log in the shade of the bushes. He was rummaging in an old bag. "Hot for this job," he said. "Need a breather."

James sat down beside him. Alf turned and eyed him again for a second, then seemed reassured and bent back to his bag. "Work up a real old sweat this weather," he said.

Behind Alf's back, James wrinkled his nose and grinned agreement. "Old sweat" just about said it all. Or "old trousers." Another smell, too—a smell which he'd rather expected. He knew what would be in the bag.

Alf righted himself. He was half-cut already. "Want a drop?"

"Cheers."

"Don't you take too much of it, mind. It . . . it'll go to your head."

"Thanks." James passed back the bottle and fished in his pocket. "Smoke, Alf?"

"Ah . . ." The eyes changed expression: the familiar glinting of greed. "Now, a gent you are. What name was it again?"

"James."

"Yes. That was it—James. A real gent you are, James."

"Go on, you might as well take a second one while you're about it, for later."

"Now, I might just do that." James made a point of not looking. Alf took his fourth cigarette. "You . . . you couldn't spare a third one, could you? I seem to have left mine back home."

"Sure. Plenty more where these came from."

"A gent you are all right, James. And don't let 'em tell you different!" The voice grew suddenly loud and bolshy. Whisky-loud. Bolshy in support of a newfound mate. James knew all the signs; was at home with them. He smoked placidly on. "Don't let 'em tell you that youngsters are no good these days. You send 'em to me if they try it on!"

"Thanks, Alf."

"You remember that, right?"

"I'll send them straight round."

"You do that. And don't you let anybody push you about, specially women."

"I don't intend to."

"That's it, you show 'em. Show 'em who's boss. That Sarah What's-her-name, wittering on about her ruddy grass. If you get fed up of her, you just come on down to my place, we'll do a bit of celebrating."

"Can I? Seriously?"

"Any time. We'll have a bit of a drink-up."

"Thanks, Alf, I might just take you up on that. You live down in the village, do you?"

"That's it."

"On your own?"

"Course on my own. Don't want women round my place, wittering on. Can't have a drink in peace. You just follow my lead and leave marrying well alone. Don't you forget that, right?"

"Don't worry, I wouldn't touch marrying if you paid me. Too much hassle."

"That's talking. Don't let 'em scare you, women. Show 'em who's boss." The loudness subsided. Alf swigged again and wiped his mouth on the back of his hand.

"Have you always been here, Alf? In the village?"

"That's it. Excepting wartime."

"Did you fight?"

"Fight? Seen it all, I have. France, Germany, all over."

"I wish I'd been around."

"Medals to prove it. And don't let 'em tell you different."

"Medals? What sort did you get?"

"All sorts. Bravery, the whole ruddy lot."

"Can I see them? When I come down?"

"Come down? Come down where?"

"You know—to your place. For the drink you said."

"Drink—yes, we'll do a bit of celebrating, have a drink-up, you and me. You just remember that, right?"

"Right. I bet you know these parts inside out, don't you, always having been here? The village and all?"

"That's it."

"And this place too, I bet."

"Know the lot. Old, this place is. Centuries."

"Georgian."

"Come again?"

"Georgian. That's what I heard, anyhow."

"Ah—that'd be it. Georgian. Old, Georgian is, like I said. Famous, this place."

"Famous?"

"Royalty's been here."

"What?"

"That Queen Elizabeth came here once. Slept here."

"You kidding?"

"Course I'm not kidding. Came on horseback, half her court with her."

"Come off it, she doesn't ride around like that. She's got a bullet-proof car."

"Not that Queen Elizabeth, you daft bugger. The first one. Henry the Eighth's time."

"Oh . . . What did she come for?"

"I told you. Slept here. Stopped off on her way somewhere. Wouldn't fancy it myself, mind, having *her* sleeping. I'd have told her to clear off somewhere else."

"Why?"

"Never had a bath, did she? I read that somewhere. Never had a bath from the day she was born. Must've stunk the place out."

James resisted the obvious comment. He stubbed out his cigarette slowly and spoke without looking up.

"From what I was hearing, this place used to be bigger than it is now. Used to be another bit on the side. But I suppose you know that?"

"Know it all."

"Was it in your time it went? The bit that's not there any more?"

"No, years ago. Years and years. Old, this place is. Georgian."

"I've often wondered what happened to the bit that's missing."

"Have you now?"

"Sure. I reckoned you might know, Alf."

"Asked what's-her-name, have you?"

"I'm not asking women."

"That's talking."

"I'm asking you."

Alf didn't answer. James sensed the eyes beside him looking shiftily at the bushes. "How about it, Alf?" With his face turned away in the other direction he put the pack of cigarettes down on the beech log between them. Then he held his breath.

Alf leaned suddenly closer, covering the pack with his palm. His whisper breathed whiskey in James's ear.

"Fire," he said.

"*Fire?*"

"Fire, that's what it was. Burnt to ruddy ashes."

"How . . . how did it happen?"

"No way of telling—"

Alf jolted abruptly to his feet. From up on the terrace a voice had come: "Alfred!"

Sarah. James got up quickly and held Alf's sleeve.

"Didn't anybody ever find out, Alf? How it happened?"

"Got to be off now."

"It won't make any odds for another couple of minutes, will it? It's only Sarah."

Alf gave a poor imitation of a jaunty wink. "Best not to cross 'em, the ladies. Best to keep on their sweet side."

"Show them who's boss, you said."

"That's it. You remember that. Show 'em who's boss."

He looked scared to death.

Sarah's voice came again. "Alfred, where are you? Your wife's on the phone."

James let go of the sleeve and stared at Alf in amazement. "Your *wife*?"

"Mustn't keep the ladies waiting. Tartars, they can be."

"Hey, you just bloody hold on! Have you been telling me the truth? About *anything*?"

"Got to go now. Keep on their sweet side."

With his bag bundled under his arm, Alf stumbled away through the bushes. James looked back round at the beech log. The cigarettes had gone.

19

"You wanted to see me, Father?"

"Yes, James. Come in and close the door. James, I am faced with something of a problem. I am hoping for your help in solving it."

"A problem, Father?"

"I am informed that certain objects have disappeared from the house. Or, to be more precise, from your bedroom."

"Objects?"

"You have no idea of the items to which I am referring?"

"No."

"Then let me list them for you in the hope that your memory may be assisted: two blankets, a pillow, two chairs and, I believe, a wooden candlestick which once belonged to your grandmother. Have you noticed their disappearance?"

"No . . . or rather, yes . . . yes, I think so."

"You think so. But you have not reported it to me?"

"Why should I have reported it?"

"I would have thought that that was obvious. Such objects hardly get up and walk. And if you tell me that you have not taken them yourself . . . you have *not* taken them yourself, have you?"

"No."

"Then that leaves only one alternative: that they have been stolen."

"Stolen? Who would want to steal them?"

"That is what we are here to find out. It will obviously be unpleasant, but we must begin with the staff."

"What?"

"Well, if you say that you had no part in the disappearance, the staff are the next line of inquiry. Are they not?"

"What . . . what are you going to do?"

"It is not what *I* am going to do, it is what *we* are going to do. We are going to interview them, one by one."

"What? I can't do that."

"And why not? I would have thought you would appreciate having the opportunity of discovering who it is who is stealing your personal property."

"And what if you—if we find out that one of them's got these things?"

"I should have thought that that, too, should be fairly evident to you. He—or she, of course—will be dismissed."

"Dismissed? Dismissed where to?"

"That is hardly our concern. Our concern is merely to find the culprit."

"Whose concern is it, then?"

"Well, that of the police, of course."

"The police?"

"The police will no doubt know how to settle the matter of thieving in their own way."

". . . Oh, all *right!*"

"All right? What is all right?"

"It *was* me. I took the things."

"I see. Then why did you lie?"

"I don't know."

"You don't know. And what have you done with these objects? Where have you taken them?"

"Out of the house."

"And why should you have wished to do that?"

"Because . . . because I wanted to set up a sort of game with them. In the garden."

"A game? With chairs and blankets? What kind of game?"

"I can't remember."

"No . . . well, perhaps you had better begin by bringing them in again, for me to see. From the—garden."

"I can't do that."

"And why can't you?"

"Because . . . because I haven't got them anymore. They got messed about and broken."

"Then you can bring the 'messed about and broken' pieces to me. Or can't you do that either?"

"No."

"You have a good explanation for that too, I presume."

"Yes. I . . . I burnt them."

"You burnt them."

"Yes. They weren't worth keeping, so I . . . so I put them on Durbon's bonfire."

"You put two blankets, a pillow, a candlestick and two chairs on the gardener's bonfire, and you burnt them."

"Yes."

"I see . . . James, there is something which I have been intending to say to you for some weeks now. Perhaps this incident will give me as good an opportunity as any. I have noticed of late that you have become increasingly disobedient."

"Disobedient? I'm not disobedient. They were my own things—you just said so. I don't see why I shouldn't be able to—"

"I am not referring to the things which were removed from your bedroom, or to the lie which you initially told me in order to free yourself from blame. I am referring to your general attitude. I have had the impression of late that you have begun to be forgetful of your position."

"What do you mean?"

"I mean your position in this household. You speak to me and to your mother with less respect and affection than you do to—to the staff, shall we say? As if—"

"Don't they deserve respect, then?"

"As if, in the past weeks, some bad influence had entered the house and were beginning to have its effect on you."

"I . . . I don't understand. What bad influence?"

"That is for you to tell me. Can you suggest what such an influence might be?"

"No."

"Then what *I* suggest is that you should attempt to discover what it might be, for yourself, and that you should be rid of it."

"There isn't any—"

"If you should fail to do so, I should of course be obliged to discover it for myself. And be rid of it, for myself. You understand me, I hope?"

"No."

"That is a pity. I shall nonetheless allow you time to think it over. Perhaps understanding may come."

"Am I . . . am I to be punished for what I did?"

"I am not a schoolmaster, James, and I do not intend to begin behaving like one. You will think over what I have said. Will you not?"

"Yes."

"Thank you, James. I shall leave you to do so."

20

"Don't swat at it, James," Sarah said. "It's smelt the stewed plums, that's all. It won't sting if you don't swat."

"It nearly settled. I didn't want to eat it, did I?"

The wasp zoomed off to the dining room window, then homed in again on the lunch table. James watched it alight on the edge of his great-uncle's dish where the old man had laid his extracted plum pits, as neat as a row of brown teeth. His great-uncle ate on unconcerned, his spoon and his fork probing the flesh of the fruit with the skill of a surgeon.

"I've got some more plums ready-cooked out in the kitchen when you've finished those, James. Do say if you'd like them."

"No thanks."

When he looked back, his great-uncle, still chewing, was dabbing his mouth on his napkin, with a smile of private contentment. James glanced at the edge of the dish and felt himself shiver; there was no sign now of the wasp.

"It's all right, James," Sarah said.

"What?"

"It's all right—the wasp's gone now. I think it went out in the hall."

"You reckon?"

He went on with his own plums in silence.

In another few minutes lunch would be over. If he wanted to ask his question, he had better be getting a move on. He spoke casually, still looking down at his spoon.

"Is this place famous?"

As he'd expected, it was Sarah who answered.

"I'm sorry, James?"

"Greville Lodge. Is it famous?"

"Famous? How do you mean?"

"You know—famous. I mean, has anybody visited it or anything?"

"Visited it? I'm not quite sure I—"

"Well, royalty or anybody?"

"What kind of royalty?"

"I don't know, do I? That's what I asked for. I thought royalty might've been here if it was famous. Queen Elizabeth the First or somebody."

"Queen Elizabeth the First?" His great-uncle's voice now, with a nasty note of amusement.

"I just wondered, didn't I?"

The thin voice went on. "I am not sure that Greville Lodge is quite grand enough to attract visits from royalty. And Queen Elizabeth in particular might have found the journey here a somewhat—demanding one."

"So she never came here, then?"

"No, as far as I am aware we have never had any sightings of ghosts here, royal or otherwise."

"What d'you mean, ghosts?"

"Greville Lodge was built in 1782, James. My memory may of course be failing me but—as I recall—Queen Elizabeth the First died in 1603. Well now, if we have all finished, I shall say grace."

The old man rose and left them. James watched him go. He felt viciously angry: with Alf, for having taken him for a sucker; with himself, for having laid himself open to his great-uncle's sarcastic comments; and with Sarah as well, for having been there to see it. And, behind his anger, there was something else too, like a feeling of apprehension brought on by the old man's words. As if, somewhere he couldn't remember, he had heard a thin cold tone like that before . . .

"Well, there now, James," Sarah said kindly, "I've learned something. Haven't you?"

"What?"

"I said I've learned something. About history. Always muddled me, history did, all those kings and queens with their dates and everything. Still, we can't all be expected to know things like that, can we?"

"Who said I didn't know?"

"Oh . . . well, I didn't say you didn't, James. Maybe it was just a bit of misunderstanding—about Queen Elizabeth, I mean."

"She was just an example, wasn't she?"

"Yes . . . yes, maybe your great-uncle didn't quite see that." She eased back her chair and began to stack up the plates on a tray. "You've got to make a few allowances for people when they get older, James. Your great-uncle meant no harm, I'm sure. And it's nice for him, I expect, feeling he can still be right about a bit of history."

"You always reckon he's right then, do you?"

"No, of course I don't. But he's usually right about things like that. Now, I must see to these lunch things."

James didn't answer, or make any offer to help her. She was getting too clever, trying to have the last word. He bit back his growing anger.

Her voice came again, smiling, smoothing things over. Her wet voice.

"Well now," she said, "fancy that. I'm going to be a soldier."

"What?"

"I'm going to be a soldier. Eleven plum pits on my dish here: tinker, tailor, soldier, sailor, rich man, poor man, beggarman, thief; tinker, tailor, soldier. Eleven. I always like to count them. Let's see what your great-uncle's going to be, shall we? Then we'll count yours."

Bloo-dy-hell. James's fingers tightened on the cloth. He stared rigidly down at his dish. How old did she think he was? Then, slowly, his face changed expression. He inched his hand sideways, and slipped one of his plum pits into his palm.

"Rich man," Sarah said. "Your great-uncle's going to be a rich man."

"You don't say?"

"What about you? Shall we see?"

"If you like. You'll have to do it for me, though. I don't know how it goes."

"Don't you, James? I thought everybody did. Now, how many plum pits have you got?"

"Eight."

"Eight. Let's see, then . . ."

"What's up? The suspense is killing me. What am I going to be?"

"I-I'm not sure. It's so silly, I've gone quite blank. I-I seem to have forgotten the rhyme."

"Pity, that," James said. "When it comes back to you, you just let me know, OK?"

He gave her a grin and left.

♦   ♦   ♦   ♦

"James . . . James . . ."

The voice was an urgent whisper. It came from the bushes. James hurried across the lawn.

Ben drew him in quickly, out of the sunlight.

"Sorry, James. Nobody's seen me, I don't reckon. Only I'm supposed to be working."

"What is it, Ben? What's happened?"

"Nothing yet. It's what's going to, maybe. I thought you might've heard different or something, I thought old Durbon might've got it wrong. I was hoping, anyhow."

"Got what wrong?"

"About the shoot."

"Shoot? I don't know what you—"

"Old Durbon told the gardening staff this morning. Said your father had given him orders, owing to the trees being damaged and all."

"Orders? What orders?"

"Six guns, he said. Eight with you and your father."

"*Me?* But I haven't heard—"

"You haven't? Let's just be hoping he *has* got it wrong then, old Durbon."

"Got *what* wrong, Ben? What am I supposed to be shooting?"

"Squirrels, from what he was saying. Those were the orders. Squirrel-shoot."

◆　◆　◆　◆

Sarah's screams reached James in his bedroom.

He jolted awake and blinked in alarm at the late afternoon sunlight. Then he realized what he was hearing. He slumped back down on the bedspread, sobbing with laughter.

She must have found it. Opened her handbag and found

it. He wished he could see. They'd be down there now, both of them, hopping and leaping all over the kitchen, as scared and as green as each other.

He buried his face in the pillow.

If she screamed at the poor little sod for much longer, it might turn into a prince.

21

James took a deep breath and spoke across to the raised copy of *The Times*.

"Can I interrupt you, Father?"

The Times resisted for a moment, then fell away.

"Of course, James . . .

"May I continue reading my newspaper, James, while you remember what it is you wished to say?"

"I . . . I'm sorry. I was thinking."

"About what you came to say to me, or about something entirely different?"

"About what I came to say."

"Then perhaps you could try thinking aloud."

"You see, I heard there was going to be a shoot. I was told the squirrels were going to be killed."

"And who told you that?"

"Isn't it true, then?"

"Perfectly true. But I asked you who told you."

"I . . . I'm not really sure. Durbon, I think."

"I don't remember suggesting to him that he should tell you. I was looking forward to giving you the news myself. I must have a word with him."

"No—no, it mightn't have been Durbon. I can't really recall."

"I see. So, you know that there is to be a shoot. Is that what you wished to tell me?"

"Yes. Well, no. I mean, not just that. I was wondering if we could . . . well, not have it."

"James, would it be possible for you to make your statements a little more clearly? And without stammering?"

"I'm sorry. I . . . I get muddled."

"James, please speak out."

"All right, I will then. I don't want this shoot to happen . . .

"Aren't you going to say anything, Father?"

"Forgive me, I hadn't realized that you had already finished. Statements of that kind are usually accompanied by an elucidation."

"Sorry?"

"A clarification, James. A reason. Have you a reason?"

"It doesn't seem fair, that's all."

"Fair?"

"They're not hurting anybody, are they?"

"On the contrary. They are hurting me."

"You, Father?"

"And I would have hoped that you would by now have developed enough sense of responsibility to see that they are also hurting you."

"Me? I don't see—"

"They are seriously damaging our trees. Destroying them. Does that mean nothing to you?"

"Yes. But they don't *know* they're doing it, do they? I mean, it's not deliberate."

"James, I confess that I have been a little short of sleep of late and am therefore slightly tired—"

"Sh-short of sleep, Father?"

"—so I am no doubt somewhat slow on the uptake. Perhaps you would be patient with me, and explain how what you have just said improves the situation of the trees?"

"Well, it doesn't, I suppose. But it can't be so bad that we've got to kill them, can it?"

"Have you seen the damage that they have already done to the bark?"

"No, but—"

"Then I would suggest that you go and inspect it. It would perhaps have been sensible to have done so before coming here to discuss the matter. You surely realize that the timber here is valuable?"

"Well, so are the squirrels, aren't they?"

"I can assure you that I have no intention of making money out of squirrels—"

"I . . . I didn't mean like that."

"Then how did you mean?"

"I can't explain very well really, Father. It's just that—well, they're more *alive* than the trees, somehow."

"I could hardly agree more. They will certainly be very much more alive than the trees soon if we fail to stop them. That is the reason for the shoot."

"It seems so cruel—"

"You puzzle me, James. Why this sudden and extraordinary concern for rodents?"

"They're not rodents!"

"Then perhaps you would care to offer another definition."

"Well—no. I just mean that they're not . . . well, rats or something."

"But that is precisely what they are: tree-rats. Or are you allowing yourself to be deceived by their pretty tails? When we last spoke together, James, I had occasion to mention a change I had noticed in you. Am I to presume that all this silly sentimentality is yet another symptom of it?"

"I'm not silly and sentimental, and I haven't changed—there's nothing wrong with me! I've never felt happier in my whole life!"

"I see. And to what can we attribute this sudden—happiness? . . . Very well, let me repeat the question which I put to you a moment ago. Perhaps it is connected. Why this sudden concern for *rodents*? You have never objected to shoots in the past."

"I haven't had to be involved in them before, have I?"

"So the informant whose name you now fail to recall told you that too?"

"Yes, I suppose so. I *am* expected to be on the shoot, aren't I?"

"Of course. That is why I was hoping to give you the news of it myself. I fondly imagined that your first engagement of this kind would give you pleasure."

"Well, it doesn't. I don't want to be there."

"You realize, of course, that that is hardly a responsible attitude? If a task such as this is required of the staff, the least we can do is to set an example. It is the first time I have asked such a thing of you, but you are surely old enough now to—"

"Who else is going to be there?"

"The gardening staff, as I have already said, eight guns in all. All the men available."

"The men? Does that include Ben?"

"Ben?"

"The . . . the new boy."

"The new boy is hardly a man."

"Well, nor am I."

"You see no difference between your own position in this household and that of a junior member of the gardening staff? Or is it simply that you would appreciate the involvement of someone of your own age in the shoot? I confess that it had not crossed my mind until now that he might join us, but I would be happy to arrange—"

"No!"

"Then I fail to see the point of your question concerning him."

"There wasn't one. I wasn't asking for anyone of my own age to be there. I don't want to be there either, I'd hate it. I *can't* shoot them, Father."

"That, as you well know, is nonsense. You have had perfectly good tuition."

"That was only targets, and . . . and I didn't mean that anyway. I meant I don't *want* to shoot them."

"I am afraid that we have no other alternative."

"You just want me to have to do it, don't you? You just want me to go out there and kill them!"

"Of course, James. That is the whole point of having a shoot."

"What if . . . what if I refuse?"

"Refuse?"

"Yes. What if I refuse to go out there? You can't make me!"

"I agree entirely."

"What? What do you mean?"

"I mean exactly what I say. I cannot make you. It would, after all, hardly be fitting for me to be seen to carry you bodily into the copse."

"So you don't mind if I don't come?"

"I mind very deeply. As it was to be your first such engagement and I have already given word to that effect to the head gardener, I would be extremely disappointed."

"I'm sorry, Father."

"Yes, I am sorry myself. But perhaps, when you have reflected on the consequences of such a decision, you may still change your mind."

"Consequences? How . . . how do you mean? Do you mean I am going to be punished?"

"I have told you before that I am not in the business of punishment."

"What consequences, then?"

"I was speaking purely selfishly. It is simply that your decision not to make up one of the party at this stage would cause me a little inconvenience."

"Inconvenience? I don't see——"

"As I said, my instructions have now been issued. I would therefore be obliged to look elsewhere for an eighth man."

"But you said all the available men were already . . ."

"Exactly. It would be inconvenient. But I would no doubt resolve the problem somehow—were it to arise. As it happens, something you yourself said a moment ago might prove the solution if need be."

"Something I . . . Father, who would it be?"

"Surely, James, that need hardly concern you——"

"Who would it be, Father?"

"—and there is no need, even for me, to come to any final decision at this stage. After all, you may still change your mind. May you not?"

". . . All right."

"I am sorry, James? I didn't quite catch your remark."

"I said, all right."

"All right?"

"I'll do it. I'll come on the shoot."

"You have really decided to join us?"

"Yes."

"Well, I must confess that I am surprised. I did trust, of course, that you would make the right decision eventually, but why so promptly?"

"To save you—inconvenience, Father."

"You will not regret it. You will enjoy the experience immensely."

"Yes. I'll go to my room now."

"Of course . . . oh, and James—"

"Yes?"

"I am grateful to you."

"For what?"

"For saving me inconvenience. And for being so—honest with me."

"I'm glad."

"It occurs to me under the circumstances—as a mark of my gratitude for your honesty, shall we say?—that I shall allow you the privilege which is traditionally reserved for me. I shall give the head gardener instructions to that effect."

"Privilege? What . . . what privilege?"

"Of opening the shooting, James. The privilege of having the first shot."

22

Ten o'clock. Even out here on the terrace the air was clogged with heat, as if the dusk wasn't real dusk at all but only thick gray sunlight, too thick and gray to breathe. James stood slumped against the house front, drained of energy and movement. He felt trapped.

He listened to the dusty thump of moths against the window of the study just beside him. His great-uncle was still in there. Sarah's light was out, though. She'd already gone to bed.

He frowned. "What the hell's she playing at?"

She hadn't mentioned the frog in her handbag. Not once. He'd been expecting her to, but she hadn't. She'd been quiet at supper, and green round the gills, and she'd not looked straight at him. But she hadn't let on that she'd found it, not even to his great-uncle. Maybe she'd given the old bloke some other excuse for her screaming? Or maybe she hadn't been sure it was James who had done it? But even Sarah couldn't be *that* thick. So what was her game?

James frowned again and idly prodded his arm with the dart-spike.

Maybe she'd written instead. That was more likely. A sneaky letter to slime-slicker Dawes. *Dear Mr. Dawes, we can't cope any longer with J. E. Greville. We never wanted him here in the first place. So just get him out of our house.* Two days, maybe, and the car would be back here, to cart him away. So what? Just see if *he* cared. For their information, J. E. Greville wasn't intending to hang around much longer in *this* dump. J. E. Greville was intending to get the hell out. He could get out right now if he wanted. There was nothing to stop him. He could have gone days ago. So why was he hanging about?

Why *was* he still here? Lack of cash, maybe? Or maybe this heat had just sapped him? Or . . .

He'd been dreaming again. He was suddenly sure he'd been dreaming this afternoon, up on his bed, before she'd yelled out. Dreaming of what, though? Anyhow, what if he *had* been? Enough to start anyone dreaming, this place. If he got out, he might be shot of his dreaming for good.

He let his eyes drift outward. The dusk had deepened into darkness. It had drained the garden dry of color. The beech copse and the grove were hardly more than shadows. There were only grays left now.

He felt suddenly lonely.

A sound inside the study brought him up abruptly. A sound as if a drawer had been pulled open. He wavered for a moment, then edged along the wall towards the window. He looked in.

He could see his great-uncle in profile. At his desk near the window, looking down at something laid before him. Not touching, just sitting and looking, with his hands on the desk-top palms downward, one on each side of whatever it was.

Moths tapped at the glass like gloved fingers. The old man didn't look up.

The hands crept slowly inward. The knuckles caught the lamplight. Then they paused again, resting on the desk-top, still not making contact with the thing that lay between them.

James inched closer. Something smallish, rectangular, block-shaped, inside a brown rubber band. He held his breath, waiting.

One hand moved, touching. The thumb stroked gently upward. The little rectangle responded, stirring as the thumb caressed its side.

James drew back. He could hear his own heart beating, louder than the moth wings. He was sure what it must be: the only thing it could be. An inch-thick bundle. An inch-thick wad of bills.

Money.

Sweat spidered down his backbone. He looked again.

The desk-top was empty. The hands had dropped down to a drawer now. From the old man's waistband a thin chain glinted, ending in a key ring. A lock clicked shut.

James pressed his forehead on the brickwork. He felt stifled. He'd been given a way out. If he wanted, he could . . .

All he had to do was get the key ring. If he did the job at night, he'd be a hundred miles away before they'd even missed him.

They'd never catch him. With that amount of cash he could lose himself in Liverpool or Sheffield, change his name, go into hiding, they'd never trace him ever, he'd be shot of them for good.

Shot of all of them. The whole lousy shambles. Shot of social workers, shot of his great-uncle, and of Sarah. And even of . . .

A new thought came. Its sudden coming choked him. He couldn't go. Not yet. He'd just remembered.

His mother.

If he went, he'd never know. She might come to. She might wake up. . . .

His fist contracted on the dart. The dart she'd bought him.

She might wake up and want him. Maybe she'd always wanted him, even if she'd never really shown it.

There was money in that drawer, more money than he'd ever even dreamed of. He could take it. But he couldn't go, not knowing if . . .

He couldn't go, not knowing.

He couldn't bloody go.

He couldn't go.

He was trapped.

Slowly, James raised his face from the brickwork. His forearm was flat against the house front. It looked pale in the darkness. Pale gray. He laid the dart against it and edged it gently upward. The tip caught at the skin.

The little fold of flesh began to tighten, resisting the bluntness. He pressed again.

The dart eased inward, metal under skin. He held it there, and waited.

His lip twisted up into a grin.

There was no more pain now. No more hurting.

He tugged out the spike, and watched the tiny movement growing. Along the gray length of his forearm, the blood slid black.

23

"You will kindly fire the first shot, James."

"Please don't make me, Father. Can't somebody else—"

"James, I have given the order. We are waiting for you to fire first."

"Please—"

"You will shoulder your gun, and fire."

Punishment. His, the first shot. They were all waiting. Faces. Guns growing out of faces. Eyes watching. Only Ben not looking, eyes bent to his gamebag, waiting too. And only the squirrels moving, not understanding. No sound but them, and the thin quiet voice above him.

"James, everyone is watching. Is it your deliberate intention to show me disobedience in front of my staff?"

"Father, please—"

"Or are you doing it to impress them?"

"What?"

"I am not prepared to wait for very much longer. James, do you wish me to—dismiss them?"

"Dis-dismiss them, Father?"

"Yes. Dismiss them, James. *Send them back.*"

"What . . . what do you mean? Send who back? Back where?"

"You are leaving me no other option."

"Back where, Father?"

"I am sure you understand my meaning. *Do* you wish me to dismiss them, James?"

"No. Please—"

"Then perhaps you will kindly do as I ask."

For an instant, Ben's eyes looked up. There was pain in them. James clenched his own eyes shut, trying not to see.

"Father, I can't."

"You will shoot, James."

"I can't."

"You will shoot. Now."

"*I can't.*"

"*Now.*"

James swung the barrel skyward.

The explosion was inside him first, inside his head and stomach like a crimson ball of anger, then it burst across his eardrums and was outside in the screaming crash and flutter of the trees.

"Thank you, James."

Then nothing but the noise and his finger on the trigger. Pulling, pulling, pulling, tearing holes out of heaven.

24

James crouched in the long grass, watching.

The blackbird was as rigidly still as he was, with its head cocked round at an angle as if it was listening. The only movement was in its eye. A fidgety, probing movement. A restless exploring of each hidden crevice.

Less than two feet away from it, James watched on.

The probing stopped. The fly squeezed itself backwards out of the eyehole spiked last week by the dart from the attic. Slowly scything its legs together, it sunned itself on the rotting skull.

25

James's father raised his eyes from his paper. James followed their direction, behind him to the doorway of the drawing room where Clara had just entered. She looked nervous.

"Excuse me, sir. There's a message—for Master James, sir. Said could he speak to him specially, at once."

"Speak to him? Who?"

"Ben, sir. From the garden. Said he'd wait outside the kitchen."

For a fraction of a second, his father didn't answer. "Thank you, Clara. That will be all. He will be there directly."

Clara backed out quickly. There was a moment of deep silence.

James caught his father's eye, and left the room.

Ben was waiting just outside the kitchen entrance, half-hidden by the laurels. James closed the door behind him.

"Ben, what is it? Father was there. He heard—"

"I'm sorry, James, honest to God I'm sorry. But I had to see you. There wasn't anybody else that could help. Can you come round here? I can't move any closer."

"Ben, what's happened?" James moved out behind the bushes. His stomach felt the impact of the sight which met his eyes. "What have you *done* to yourself? You're *covered*."

"It's not me—"

"But your hands—they're bleeding. And your shirt—"

"It's all right, don't you touch me or you'll be getting it all over you—"

"I don't care about that, for God's sake—"

"It's not mine, James. Not my blood. It's Beech's."

"What?"

"Beech's. I've got him down by the lake. I had to carry him, inside my shirt. I've done what I could, like, but he's none too good."

"Beech? I don't . . ." James felt his own blood turn to ice inside him. He stared across at Ben. "It was me, wasn't it?"

"What was? James, what was?"

"I did it, didn't I? This morning . . ."

"It wasn't anything you did."

"This morning. I shot him, didn't I?"

"No. Course you didn't. He was all right dinnertime. He's not shot, he's maimed."

"What?"

"You just come, all right? I can't talk out here. Please, James. I haven't got anybody else I can ask—Midge'd talk about it after, up at the house. You will come, won't you?"

"Yes."

James followed numbly, through the garden and down into the copse. Where the trees opened out onto the lakeside, Ben stopped.

"Well, here he is. I've laid him in the moss, to be more gentle on him. Not that he'll be noticing, yet a while. Sleeping now, he is."

James stared. Something retched inside him, like fingers in his throat.

Ben knelt down. "Rotten bad luck it was really, getting clear of all that shooting and then ending up in a pickle like this. He's lost his poor old paw all right. No way of saving it, there wasn't, I had to take it off. He'd have had it off himself, anyhow, if I hadn't chanced on him."

"What . . . what happened, Ben?"

"Heard him screaming, I did. After dinner, up in the field. Sort of knew it was him. It's me I blame more than anybody. I must've missed one. One of those traps of your father's."

James froze. "It's horrible, Ben. It's . . ."

"It's not pretty, that's for certain sure."

"It's *horrible*. It's . . . it's like that poem."

"What? Oh, come on now, that's just daft talk that is. Deuced spring-traps, this was, not poems."

"*I hate him.*"

"Well, what's done's done, and it's not hating's going to help the poor little beggar now. I've staunched the bleeding as best I can, but he's lost a good drop and no mistake. I'm going to get him over to the cabin in a bit. I can't leave him over on this side—he'll try and scarper off when he comes to, and he's at risk for a while yet. From other animals and that. He'll be all right, though, I reckon, so long as the gangrene's kept out."

"Gangrene?"

"You haven't got something as might help, have you? Back at the house?"

"I . . . I don't know. I don't know anything about—"

"Spirits, they'd do, to put on where the iron's been. Filthy rusty those traps are."

"Spirits?"

"Brandy. Anything'd do."

"Yes . . . yes, all right. I'll go and get it, shall I?"

"When I get back'll be time enough."

"Back?"

"You can stay on with him, can you? Not long, it won't be. I've got to report in to Durbon and I'm late already, second time in two days. I don't want to be losing my post."

"But Durbon would understand, wouldn't he?"

"Oh, he'd understand maybe, but it'd be more than his post's worth as well as mine, saving squirrels."

"I don't . . ."

"Can't go shooting them one minute and saving them the next. Orders, isn't it?"

"You mean my father."

"You can stay, can't you?"

"Yes."

"Thanks, James. It's only to watch over him a bit. He'll be out for the count for a while, if I know anything."

Ben began to move away along the lakeside. James's voice made him turn back.

"Ben, he's not going to . . ."

"Course he's not, not old Beech. Don't you fret. Not done for by a long chalk, old Beech isn't, not if I can help it." He grinned. "More than can be said for my shirt, I reckon. Done for, good and proper, this is."

James listened to the footsteps receding through the grasses. He looked down, feeling suddenly alone. Then, slowly, he reached forward.

For a while he remained there, watching without moving, and felt the tiny heartbeat that was answering to his own.

♦　♦　♦　♦

Snip snap snip
Snip snap snip the scissors go
James was chanting. His chanting half woke him.
Snip snap snip they go so fast
That both his thumbs
He listened to the pulsing of his heartbeat. The pulsing of the words inside his head.
That both his thumbs
He'd buried it. Buried the blackbird.
Snip snap snip
Under the rubble.
The voice chanted on, in his sleep.

26

"Got you!"

It came from behind. A hand out of nowhere. It closed on his wrist like a vise.

James froze. His legs wouldn't move, to get him across to the doorway. He couldn't even turn round.

It had happened. Happened again like in London. The moment of nightmare, the moment he dreaded. He'd been through it all before.

"Got you, you ruddy little thief!"

The voice was behind him. In front of him, out by the shelves, was the startled face of the woman in the green nylon tunic. She'd frozen too, clutching a packet of tea.

Then she moved. She hurried towards him but her eyes looked straight past him, over his shoulder, to the person behind his back.

"Dad, what is it? Let him go, Dad, it's all right. He couldn't find the tea, that's all."

"Got him red-handed. Filching behind his back, he was. Filching the cigarettes."

"Now then, you let him go. I'm sure he wasn't. Come on, Dad, it's all right, let him go."

The grip fell away. James half turned. Beyond the till, an open door showed a glimpse of a parlor. So the old man had come out from there, then. A bald old man in baggy corduroy trousers, with a trembling head and eyes that were goggly and bloodshot. James recognized him at once.

"All right, Dad—"

"Watching him I was, from back there. Knew there was going to be trouble the minute I saw him come in—same little hooligan I saw the other day up on the church wall, giving me his lip. Filching cigarettes behind his back he was, while you weren't looking."

"*Were* you?" The woman faced James. She was trembling too.

"Course I wasn't."

"They're still in his ruddy hand."

"I was just getting them off the rack, wasn't I? I was going to pay for them when she got back to the till."

"I expect he was, Dad."

"What about the others, then? The ones he's already stuffed in his pockets? Going to pay for that lot too, was he?"

Silence. Too long a silence. If James had been going to talk his way out, he ought to have done it at once, without waiting. But his brain had stopped dead. It was too late now.

A sudden disturbance: the click of the shop door, the jangling noise of the bell. The till-woman moved across quickly, turning a white cardboard sign back to front on the entrance.

"I'm sorry, Mrs. Lee, Mrs. Stebbins, we're closed for just a minute. I'll be with you as soon as I can."

The door rattled shut. The bell repeated its jangle. James watched the sign saying OPEN swing to and fro on its thread. Beyond it the faces peered in through the glass, mouthing in dumb show, like faces observing a fish tank.

Like last time, James thought, and the times before that. Open for viewing. Faces peering, and him being peered at. J. E. Greville, special exhibit. Caught hook, line and sinker.

He emptied his pockets and threw the cigarettes on the till.

"I don't want the things anyway," he said. "You can keep your flaming butts."

"So you *were* stealing, then?"

"Course he was ruddy stealing."

"Now you leave this to me, Dad. You go on back into the parlor."

"I'm ringing the police, that's what I'm doing."

"Dad, you just leave it.— You were in here the other day, lad, weren't you? I remember now. You had me on the same game then too, didn't you, fetching stuff off the shelves for you? Did you take cigarettes that time as well? It's no good you just shrugging. Where are you from? Are you from round here?"

"I might be. What's that to you?"

"Here, don't you start that lip with my daughter—"

"Dad—"

"I'm staying up the bloody Lodge, OK?"

"The Lodge? Greville Lodge?" Silence again. The woman's face white and bewildered. The two other faces still nosing and craning outside the doorway. "You're . . . you're not James, are you?"

"What if I am? Heard all about me, have you?"

The woman's expression had changed now. She was bundling out of her tunic. "It's all right, Dad, he's the boy staying with Sarah, the one she mentioned. Mr. Greville's lad, come up from London for his holiday."

James heard himself snort. "Holiday? That's her story, is it?"

"What . . . what do you mean, her story? You *are* James Greville, aren't you?"

"OK. So I'm James Greville. Big deal."

"It *is* him, Dad. I'm taking him back to the Lodge, all right?"

"I don't care who he is, he wants locking up—"

"You'll leave that telephone alone. We'll talk about it when I get back."

"Ruddy little thief."

"Now stop it, or you'll make yourself poorly. I'm taking him back up to Sarah, so you can just look after the shop for a few minutes while I'm gone."

James went with her across to the doorway. The two old women scuttled aside as he passed them. He could feel their eyes on his back as he made his way through the high street, then he heard them turn round and hurry on into the shop.

He followed the till-woman slowly, a few steps behind her. She kept stopping, and waiting for him to catch up. They walked without speaking, on through the village and into the graveled driveway. Another two minutes would bring them back up to the Lodge.

He wondered what made him follow. He could give her the slip if he wanted. But he couldn't be bothered. And it made no odds now: at least it would soon all be over. Sarah would tell his great-uncle, his great-uncle would ring up the police or the Social, by tomorrow he'd be back in London. Taken into Care, he supposed, if anyone cared to take him. And if not . . .

"Come on, James, I haven't got all day."

"I'm coming, aren't I?"

"Sarah's going to be very upset about all this."

Like hell she would. Being shot of him would be the biggest break she'd had in ages. He wondered if she'd manage not to show how pleased she felt.

Their footsteps sounded loud on the driveway and the terrace, but Sarah hadn't heard them. She turned round as they came into the kitchen and looked at them, uncertain, half-smiling, half-bewildered.

"Joyce? Joyce, what is it? What's the matter?"

James hung back in the doorway as Joyce went across to her and whispered. Sarah's face turned white.

"James, it's not true, is it? There's been some mistake, hasn't there?"

James raised his eyes towards her and watched her without blinking.

"Course it's true," he said. "You needn't worry about that."

"James . . ." Sarah said. "James, why?"

Joyce had gone, and left them alone in the kitchen.

"Why did you do it?"

James didn't answer, and didn't look up. She wasn't intending to tell his great-uncle. She wasn't intending to ring up the police. So what was she playing at?

"Can't you try and tell me, James?"

What was her game? He could make a pretty shrewd guess now, and the thought of it crushed him. She did want him here after all, then. She wouldn't let on to a soul that he'd done it, any more than she'd mentioned the frog in her handbag. It'd all be their own little secret. And he'd have to keep showing how grateful he was.

"I don't like the idea of you smoking, it's so bad for you, but . . . but I'd have *bought* you a few cigarettes rather than this, you could've had a bit of money if you'd asked me."

He'd have to be nice to her, show her he liked her, he'd have to put up with her fussing and mussing. She'd got him where just she'd always wanted, and now that she'd got him she'd never let go. He felt more trapped than ever. Stifled.

"You didn't have to . . . to go and steal."

He couldn't even do *that* right, without getting nicked in the process. He was a washout.

"What's the matter, James? Can't you tell me? I could try and help, maybe."

"Who says I need help? I *don't*, OK?"

"But why did you have to go and do that?"

"Look, it was just a couple of packs of cigarettes, wasn't it? And I've given them back, haven't I?"

"I just hoped so much that coming here would make it all a bit better. And your great-uncle, too. It would make him so happy if things worked out."

"Told you that, has he?"

"I don't need telling. I've been with him for such a long long time now, and I know these things, James, without words. You shouldn't speak about him like that. He's so concerned for you."

"Funny way of showing it."

"Well, it's *his* way, the only way he's got, and we just have to try and accept it. I know he can seem a bit funny sometimes but, well, people aren't always like they seem, maybe, and . . . and he *is* concerned, underneath."

"I don't need his concern, right? I've had to manage OK without it till now, haven't I?"

"James, everybody needs—"

"I'd hardly even heard of him till I got sent here, had I? He'd never even written. He never even wrote to find out how . . . how my mother was, did he?"

"Oh, James, I know, I know. It's all been so sad. I've always wished it could've been different. But there, families can be like that sometimes, and no way of changing things. When I think of all those years and years without your great-uncle and your grandfather talking to each other . . ."

"I suppose it was my grandad's fault, was it?"

"Faults aren't ever only on the one side. Your grandfather—"

"This house was half his though, wasn't it? And he was just kicked out."

"James, that's not true. Your grandfather never wanted this house, he wanted to live down in London. And your great-uncle gave him his half-share in money, just the way your grandfather asked. It was all fair and equal, I know it was."

"So what? Makes no odds to me, does it?"

"Well, you shouldn't go saying things like that. You don't know your great-uncle. He's a bit old-fashioned maybe, that's all, and he finds it hard sometimes to go along with other people's ways."

"He didn't fancy the way my grandad went on, you mean, blowing all his cash on gambling. The same as he didn't fancy knowing my mother was boozing half her time. Ashamed of them or something, was he? That's what stopped him writing, isn't it? He didn't even show up at my gran and grandad's funeral, did he?"

"Oh, James, please don't. I told you, there are always wrongs both ways and . . . and it's not for me to be talking about it like I am. It doesn't help any. I know how hard things must have been for you at home, and I only want to—"

"How? How d'you know? You don't know anything about me, do you?"

"I know things can't have been very happy for you, that's all, but it doesn't do, always looking back."

"Who said I wasn't happy?"

"Why are you so afraid of asking for a bit of a helping hand, James? I'm only trying to—"

"I just told you, didn't I? I don't *need* any help. What d'you think I am—some sort of freak?"

"Oh, of course I don't. I can just see you're not very happy."

"OK, so I'm not happy. Satisfied now? Not likely to be either, am I, locked up in this place?"

"It's not this place you're locked up in, James, it's inside your own poor self. You're all bottled up—"

"Been listening to old Dawes or something, have you? Reading what's in my personal files?"

"—but you're not the only one. There're other people in the world who've had things hard."

"I'm going, OK?"

"James, I didn't mean to sound . . . listen, close the door up again, just for a minute. I don't want your great-uncle hearing."

"He can hear the lot, for all I care. You can go and tell him."

"I'm not going to tell him—"

"Supposed to be grateful, am I?"

"—the same way I didn't tell him what I found in . . . in my bag."

"Oh? What was that, then? Something else I'm supposed to have done, is it?"

"James—"

"If you reckon it's something I've done wrong you'd better go ahead and tell him all about it. He's the one who's supposed to be in charge of me, isn't he? It's his house, not yours."

"I don't *want* to tell him."

"Suit yourself."

"I don't want to tell him, because I don't want him upset—can't you understand that? I don't want to go hurting his feelings."

"Not much chance of that. He's got no feelings to hurt, from what I've seen."

"That's . . . that's a terrible thing to say. You don't know anything about him. You've never even tried to understand."

"Like *he's* tried with me, you mean? Made me welcome all right, hasn't he?"

"James, he *has* tried."

"You could've fooled me."

"He finds it so hard, showing things he's feeling, but it doesn't mean he doesn't care. Please try and understand him a bit. You could understand better than anybody if you'd only—"

"I'm going upstairs now, right?"

"Please listen."

"Or aren't I allowed to? Going to be kept down here in the kitchen from now on, am I, for punishment?"

"But it's nearly lunchtime. And I'd so like us all to—"

"I don't want any lunch, OK? I'm going upstairs, then I'm going out for a walk."

"Don't go yet. Don't go out. It's so hot for walking and . . . and I've done a bit of pie, specially. I thought—"

"I don't want your lousy pies. I don't want *anything*, off you or off him. I just want to be left on my own. Got it?"

"James, what can I do?"

"You can get off my flaming back."

27

He heard the sound of feet on the grass behind him. The little figure was with him almost before he'd turned round.

"Midge, what is it?"

There was no answer. Only a helpless attempt at a curtsy, and a voice that was choked with tears.

"Don't be upset, Midge. Tell me what's the matter."

"It's not true."

"What isn't?"

"It's not true what they're sayin'."

"What who's saying? Look, you tell me about it, and I'll try and help." He knelt and held her gently, his palms against her waist. "Don't cry, Midge. Please. Here, you have my handkerchief. I'm sorry it's . . . it's not very clean. Now you can tell me what's wrong, can't you?"

"He never done it, what they're sayin'."

"Who, Midge?"

"He never."

"Do you mean Ben?"

"He wouldn't."

"Wouldn't what, Midge? What are they saying he's been doing?"

"Nickin'. But he'd never."

"Stealing? Ben? Well, of course he wouldn't. *I* know that. Ben's the last person in the whole world who'd—"

James froze. And Midge's sobs stopped as abruptly as his voice had. She stared at him, alarmed.

"Master James, you all right? You all right, Master James?" She took a step backward. His palms remained where she'd left them, poised in midair, as if he'd not noticed she'd gone from between them. "You look—funny."

"What?"

"You look funny. Your eyes. You all right?"

"Yes . . . yes, I'm all right."

"You scared me."

"I—I'm sorry. Midge, listen. You said that people are saying that Ben has been stealing. Don't cry again. Please try and listen. I want to help. I've got to know."

"I've told you."

"But what are people saying he's taken, Midge? Can't you just tell me that?"

"Stuff. From the house. But he wouldn't—"

"Of course he wouldn't. What stuff, Midge?"

"Daft stuff. Chairs and stuff. And stuff of Sir's."

". . . Of Father's?"

"A bottle from out the dining room. Brandy or some such, but he'd never . . ."

"Where is he now, Midge?"

"What?"

"Where's Ben now?"

"Don't know. Sir sent Durbon off lookin', but he's not found him. He must be hidin'."

"You—you don't think he's gone, do you?"

"Gone where?"

"I mean, run away?"

"He'd never do that. Not without seein' me first. Sayin' good-bye."

The tears came back, puckering her face with pain.

"It's all right, Midge. He'll be in the garden somewhere. I'll find him."

"He's goin' to have to be sent back, isn't he?"

"*No*. I promise, Midge. So there's nothing to cry about anymore, is there?"

"You're makin' me. You're all white and funny."

"You go in now. Clara will be wondering where you've got to. I'll find him. You just leave it to me, OK?"

"Here's your hanky."

"You keep it for a bit, Midge."

"I can't."

"Of course you can."

"I don't *want* it."

"I only thought—"

"Sir'll see."

"What?"

"He'll see, and say I nicked it. Like he said with Ben. Then he'll send me back too."

She fled, and left him still kneeling, with the handkerchief flung on the grass.

28

Sarah had been right about one thing: it was too hot for walking. But James walked on, up the track that climbed the hillside. There were fields in all directions, with sheep that filled the air with bleating sounds like laughter. They fell silent when he passed them and looked at him politely, then jeered at him again behind his back. He knew the type.

Forty minutes brought him almost to the summit. When he reached it, he'd lie down and have a breather: the trees up there would give a bit of shade. He trudged on up towards them.

Apart from the sheep and the scratchy dry chirrup of insects he was all on his own here, more alone than he'd been in the whole of his lifetime. Well, he'd *wanted* to be on his own, and he was, right? But there was a difference, he thought, between feeling you wanted to be on your own, and feeling just lonely. And he felt lonely. He paused for a moment and looked back the way he had come.

The sky had lost its blueness: it was sticky gray with heat haze and the sun was just a blur now. He could see the village far away below him. At least he was shot of it till tea-time—even later if he wanted. He wished he'd brought a drink, though. He was sweltered. He supposed—if he kept going—he might reach another village and cadge a glass of water. Unless he just flaked out before he got there.

Then the dog appeared. A sheepdog. It came from out of nowhere and trotted up to join him. He'd never fancied dogs, he was scared they might leap up and gouge straight through his windpipe. He'd seen a video like that, back home in London. His hand went to his pocket, to be ready with his dart.

But the dog gave no indication of leaping. It seemed to accept him. And James felt suddenly glad of its presence. Leaving the dart in his pocket, he bent down and held out his hand. The dog didn't rip off his fingers, it licked them. Then it pricked up its ears and stood to attention: from up in the thicket a whistle had come.

The dog turned and left him. He watched it bolting away through the field to the trees at the farthermost end of the thicket. There, in the shade, was a man.

The man raised his hand briefly and waved. James didn't wave back. Now that he knew that he wasn't alone here, he felt less inclined to be friendly. If he answered the wave the bloke would be sure to come over towards him. But he'd sat down now with his back to a tree and seemed already unconscious of James's existence. Maybe he'd make no demands, then. He might be OK. And, more to the point, he seemed to be having his lunch there. Drinking . . .

James wavered a moment, then sauntered along the edge of the thicket towards him.

"Hello," the man said.

"Hello."

"Hot for walking."

"Yes."

About forty perhaps, in an open-necked shirt and old trousers. The sheep dog was stretched out beside him. The man took a swig from a can, then reached to his right and fished in a lunch box. He held out a can towards James.

"Here, you look as if you could use it. Go on, take it, I've got another couple."

"Thanks."

It was shandy. James drank, watching the man as he did so. The man didn't watch back.

"Take the weight off your legs. There's a bit of bacon sandwich here if you fancy it."

"What?"

"There's plenty. Glad of the company."

"OK. Thanks."

"Name's Jeff, by the way."

"Thanks, Jeff."

James sat down beside him, more at his ease now. The bloke was all right.

For a while they ate without speaking.

"They your sheep down there, Jeff?"

"No, over behind the thicket mine are. I've come from seeing to them. Nice bit of shade up here, for dinner-time—here, Skipper, catch." The sheepdog caught the half-sandwich and snapped it up quickly. Then it settled back down with its head on its paws.

"He's well-trained, Jeff, isn't he?"

"Needs to be for this job, sheep and everything. I couldn't manage without him. Wouldn't want to, either—good company, old Skipper is."

"He must be. It must seem lonely up here sometimes."

"Oh, doesn't bother me that much. Always things to be doing. Here, have another can."

"I . . . I don't want to put you short."

"You won't do that."

"That's dead generous. Smoke, Jeff?"

"Not for me. Don't want to be dying yet a while, thanks all the same."

James stuffed the unopened packet back in his jeans and picked up the shandy. "Cheers, Jeff. Just what I needed, this is. It's a longer walk up here than I reckoned."

"Not from round these parts, then?"

"No . . . no, I'm just visiting for the holidays. I'm staying with my gran and grandad."

"Local people, are they?"

"Not really, they haven't been here long. They've bought a cottage up here to sort of retire to."

"Which village would that be, then?"

"You first. Which village are you from?"

"Oh, Barnford folk we are. Three or four miles up over the hill there."

"You probably wouldn't know Gran and Grandad, then. They're down there. Little Aston."

"No, I'd doubt we'd know them. What name would it be?"

". . . Lewis. Mr. and Mrs. Lewis."

Jeff shook his head. "No, we don't see much of Aston folk up Barnford way. Nice little village it is, though, what I know of it.. See your cottage from here, can you?"

"I don't reckon."

"Hard to make out from this distance, it'd be, you've come a good step. That'll be Greville Lake down on the left there, where it's shining. Or the duck-pond it could be. There's a pub by the pond I used to go to off and on in the old days."

"The Swan."

"That's the one. That's about all I know of Aston."

"You . . . you don't know Greville Lodge, then?"

"I know of it. I've never been there, though. You know it, do you?"

"No, not really."

"Old, Greville Lodge is. Must go back a century or two."

"Wasn't . . . wasn't there a fire there once?"

"A fire? Now, there might've been, now you come to say it."

"Was it a bad one?"

"I couldn't rightly tell. Before my time, that'd have been. Your grandad might know."

"Who?"

"Your grandad. He might've heard, being in Aston."

"Oh . . . oh yes. I'll maybe ask him."

"Yes, old family the Grevilles were. Just the two sons eventually, as I recall. The younger one got married and went off down south somewhere, but I don't know what became of him. It was the older brother who was living there when I used to go down to the Swan. Funny old bloke by all accounts."

"Funny?"

"Kept himself to himself. Not the pub-going sort, like. Mind you, he was a bit crippled in the legs from what I've heard, so maybe that's why."

"Got smashed up in the war, did he?"

"May have been that. But no, before that it was, I'd guess. Here—a bit more bacon sandwich?"

"Thanks."

"Your mum and dad up here on holiday as well?"

"What?"

"Your mum and dad. Come up here with you, have they?"

"Oh, no. Dad's . . . Dad's in the army. He's a major, actually, armored division. He's over in Germany at the moment on maneuvers."

"Is he now? Well, well. Not that I've ever held with all this warring and fighting myself, I must admit. More for the quiet life I am. But it's a job that's got to be done, I suppose, and I admire them that's prepared to do it."

"Me too. Dad's a really great bloke."

"You reckoning on following in his footsteps, are you? Joining up?"

"You bet. I've flown over there to see him a couple of times, where he's based and everything, and he reckons he can fix it OK if that's what I'm set on."

"Well, it's good to see you've got things all mapped out, I'll say that. I've always been the same myself. Farming it was with me. Happy as a sandboy I am when I'm out here. Same with the wife, Barnford born and bred and wouldn't change it for the world."

"Got any children?"

"Oh yes, there's the daughter. Married now, but still just round the corner. No, the army life wouldn't do for me, always upping sticks and off to Germany and places. Homesick I'd be for sure, and wanting the family. But there, each to his own. You must miss him though, your dad, mustn't you?"

"Yes . . . yes, I do. But he writes to me every day, never fails. Real letters, mind, not just postcards and stuff."

"Does he now? Well, must make up for a lot, that must. You want to keep all those letters for when you're grown up. Something to be proud of one day they'll be, and no mistake."

"Yes."

"And your mum's over with him, is she? In Germany?"

"Oh . . . oh no, she's over here. She wouldn't go off and leave me."

"No, course she wouldn't. She got a job too, has she?"

"She works with computers, stuff like that."

"Computers, does she? Well. Must be a clever one all right. Never fathomed them myself, computers. But I expect you understand all about them, do you, having a mum like that?"

"Well, she's teaching me. We do a bit in the evenings, every day when she comes home from work."

"Now that's good, that is. Good for her too, I don't doubt, what with your dad away. You must be real close, you and her."

"Yes."

"And you've got your own computer then, have you? At home, like?"

"Yes, she bought me one last Christmas."

"Well, fancy that. Buying you your own computer."

"She's always buying me stuff, Mum is."

"Is she now?"

"Cassette-players, videos, all sorts of stuff."

"Well, fond of you all right, she must be."

"Yes . . . she . . . she bought me this, too."

"What've you got there, then? Oh . . . looks just like an old dart to me."

"Yes."

"Well, now. A dart. I thought I was going to be seeing a computer for a minute, the way you were talking. Still . . . a present from your mum, you say?"

"Yes."

"Well, there then. Some special sort of dart though, I expect, is it?"

"No. No, it's just an ordinary one."

James got up and put the dart back in his pocket. He turned away and stood staring out with his hand across his eyes.

"Mind you," Jeff said, "I didn't mean . . . It looks a good dart, that does."

"Yes. Thanks for the shandy, Jeff. I've got to be going now."

"Have you? Well, it's been a real treat talking to you. You . . . you all right, son, are you?"

"Yes, I'm OK. It's this bloody hay fever, that's all. It . . . it gets me in the eyes. Comes on dead sudden sometimes."

"Hay fever, is it? Bad luck that is, hay fever. Now you just wait a tick, I've got a bit of paper towel in my tin here somewhere."

But James had already gone.

29

There was a rustle in the grove.

James tensed, and crouched down lower in the grove rushes by the lakeside. He held his breath and listened. The sound had gone now, everything was silent. As if the night had held its breath, and listened back.

Then another rustle, nearer.

A footstep?

Please let it be him, and not my father—

A twig cracked, like a gunshot. He clenched his eyes in panic.

When he opened them again he saw a figure creeping forward, out into the moonlight on the shore.

"Ben."

At James's sudden movement, Ben stopped dead.

"Ben . . . it's only me."

"James?"

"I didn't mean to scare you. It's all right, Ben, nobody knows I'm here. I—I've been waiting."

"But how did you know I'd come here?"

"I just guessed, that's all."

"How long have you been waiting?"

"I don't know. An hour, I suppose."

"An hour?"

"Or two, maybe. I don't know. I came out after Father went to bed. I just wanted to see you, and . . . I didn't know what to do, Ben. And I thought you might need somebody to—to talk to a bit."

"You've heard, then?"

"Yes."

Ben was silent, gazing out across the lake towards the island. James watched him. He wanted to move forward, to go and stand beside him. But something seemed to tell him that Ben was out of reach now. Something in the eyes, he thought, like loneliness, or sadness.

Ben turned to him and smiled. The smile made his eyes look sadder still.

"Thanks for coming, James."

"Where have you been hiding?"

"All over, I reckon. Moving about, like. In the copse for a bit, then up top-field. Stopped hunting for me, have they?"

"I think so."

"Thought they would, come nighttime. Starting it up again early tomorrow, are they?"

"I don't know. He doesn't tell me anything. I found out from Midge."

"She's heard too, then?"

"Yes."

"How did she take it? . . . It's all right, James, you don't have to say it. I know, without saying."

"Listen, Ben—if we can talk it over a bit, maybe it won't seem so bad. That's why I wanted to see you. To find the best way out. I mean, you haven't done anything wrong. You didn't take the things—"

"I've still got them though, over on the island. Comes to the same."

"But it doesn't. You didn't take them, *I* did. I'm going to tell him, Ben, first thing tomorrow."

"It'd make no difference, telling. I'd be sent back just the same."

"Don't say that. You can't be sent back if he can't prove anything. I'll tell him it was me who took the stuff—"

"And what's he going to say when you tell him why?"

"I—I won't tell him that. I can make something up. I can make him believe the stuff was for me."

"Like he believed you the last time? It's no good you lying to him, James. It'll only get you in trouble same as me. He'll find out in the end. Worse then it'll be, for both of us."

"He won't find out. I'll tell him that I—"

"And what am I going to tell him?"

"What?"

"What am I going to tell him? When he asks me why I've been hiding away from him? See me lying to him as well, can you, and him not finding out? I can't think straight even now, James. I'm all muddled in my head."

James didn't answer. There were no answers anymore. He felt Ben's eyes on him. He didn't turn to meet them.

"Don't you fret, James. It'll be all right, I reckon. I'll get away."

"Yes."

"They maybe reckon I've cleared out already, what with hunting the grounds and not finding me. Safest place, this is, to lie low a while—on the island, like."

"How long will you stay?"

"A day or two, maybe, to try and get my muddles sorted out. And . . . well, I can't go just yet."

"I know."

He heard the sudden smile in Ben's voice. "That's how you guessed then, is it? That I'd stay on a bit, and come here tonight? To the raft?"

"Yes."

"He's mending well, James. Real friendly now, he is. In a day or two he'll be back to his old self, near enough. Once he can cope with the climbing, up the pine trees and that, I'll bring him back over. You'll maybe see to him when I'm gone? A few hazels, like, come dinnertime?"

"Yes."

"Well . . . I'd best be getting across now, then."

"Don't take the raft, Ben."

"What?"

"Don't take the raft. I'll need it. I can't swim."

"Swim?"

"You'll want food if you're staying."

"I—I can go without, for a day or two."

"I'll come across."

"James, I don't want you getting yourself caught."

"I'll come across. Tomorrow night."

"Your father . . ."

"And I'll rustle up some hazels."

Ben stripped off his clothes and buckled them up tightly in his oilskin kitbag. He paused for a moment, and held out his hand.

"Thanks, James."

He waded out, thigh-deep. Turning to the shore, he raised his arm above him. Then he curved like a fish into the water of the lake.

30

James opened his eyes. There was shadow on them, the shadow of his dreaming. He reached out to hold it, to stop it slipping from him. But the dream, when he clutched it, was empty in his fingers, and the shadow just the shadow of long grass.

He sat up and looked around. He was alone.

He was sitting by a hedgerow at the corner of a meadow. For a moment he wondered how he'd got here. Then he remembered: it was after he'd left Jeff; he'd run in here and thrown himself full-length among the grasses. There'd been sheep in the next field, but they'd all gone now, and the thicket on the skyline showed no sign of either Jeff or of the sheepdog. They must have gone while he'd been sleeping. He blinked down at his watch. It was half past five.

He ought to go himself. But his head and limbs felt heavy, as if his dreams were still inside them. He frowned in concentration, trying to recall them, but the effort seemed to bury them still deeper. He gave it up and struggled to his feet.

It was hotter now than ever. There was no breath of movement and the sky looked thick and scummy. He plodded down the track towards the village, letting his legs take him. Maybe this was how it felt to be walking in your sleep. *He* ought to know. He'd done it enough times, from what they'd told him back in London. Or maybe they'd been lying, just saying it to scare him. He wouldn't put it past them.

Another twenty minutes brought him nearly to the driveway.

He wished he *was* just walking in his sleep. All this would be a dream then. Or a nightmare. Sarah, his great-uncle, the whole lousy setup. He turned in at the gates and pushed on up the gravel. The lawns now, and the terrace. He paused before the house front. This wasn't any nightmare. It was worse: it was real.

The house closed round him.

Sarah was standing in the passage. She looked as if she'd been there ever since he'd left her.

"I'm back," he said.

"Yes. Can you go to the study, James?"

"What?"

"The study. Your great-uncle's there. He'd like a bit of a word with you."

"What about?"

"He's . . . he's been waiting."

James watched her. Her eyes were red and puffy. They didn't meet his own.

So she'd talked then, after all. She'd blabbed about this morning. He wavered for a moment, then walked past her.

The study door was open. He took a step inside and waited, his hand still on the doorknob. His great-uncle turned towards him from the sofa. He looked tired.

"I was told you wanted to see me."

"Yes. Come in, James. Close the door. I have some news for you, James. Would . . . would you care to come a little nearer?"

"I'm OK over here, thanks."

"Yes. Yes, as you please."

James waited again. There was silence. And suddenly he knew that he'd guessed wrong: he wasn't here to talk about his stealing. The news the old man had was something different. He could feel it hanging in the empty space between them, still unspoken. . . . The doorknob was cold in his fingers. He felt a desperate need to turn it. To get out.

"James, while you were away I made a telephone call. To the hospital . . . did you say something, James?"

"No."

"I thought perhaps I should inform you of the news which I have been given. You must understand that I did not speak directly with . . . with your mother, but only with the doctor under whose care she has been placed. The information which I have received is that her condition is, as the doctor expressed it, satisfactory. Doctors are inclined to be somewhat guarded in what they say, but I am sure that you can nevertheless appreciate what such a statement implies."

"N-no."

"No. As you say, it is always difficult to interpret such things with any assurance, but I think we may safely assume that her condition is—stable."

"What?"

"She is not . . . she is not as had been feared."

"D'you mean she's—all right?"

"It would be safe, certainly, to say that much. She is—out of danger. James, you should, I think, sit down. You look—"

"I'm OK."

"Or perhaps you would prefer to go upstairs for a while? I realize that the—"

"I'm OK."

"Yes. I hope at least that the news may set your mind at rest somewhat. It must have been an anxious time—"

"She's . . . she's conscious and everything?"

"Forgive me, I thought I had made that clear. Yes, she is conscious. She has been so for some time, I gather—for some thirty-six hours."

"So she knows about me? Where I am?"

"Certainly. She has been informed of . . . of what has happened, and of the arrangement which has been made for you. And she would appear to have expressed acceptance of it."

"She can talk a bit, then?"

"She is talking perfectly well, it seems. You need trouble yourself no further on that score—she is quite rational. Well, that is the information, James. I am sure that you would like the opportunity of being on your own for a while, to appreciate it fully."

"Is . . . is that all?"

"I am sorry, James, I don't quite—"

"All the news? I mean, wasn't there anything about . . . about me?"

"About you? James, as far as your own situation is concerned . . . yes, there is something that should perhaps be made clear. I was not intending that it should be discussed immediately, but as you yourself have raised it . . . James, your mother's recovery has obviously been a matter of some satisfaction to everyone concerned, but . . . but it must remain doubtful whether—if ever—she will improve sufficiently to take complete responsibility for herself again. As for—"

"I didn't mean that."

"—as for her taking responsibility for . . . for anyone else—"

"I meant, wasn't there any message?"

"James, have you heard what I have been saying?"

"Yes."

"Then it must be clear to you that we must try to accept that there is little hope of you ever—"

"Wasn't there any message? For me?"

"I am sorry, James, I didn't quite catch what you said."

"I said, wasn't there any message for me?"

"It is early days yet, of course . . ."

"Didn't she . . . didn't she say she wanted to see me?"

"James, she should not perhaps be troubled at present with—"

"But didn't she say she wanted to see me?"

"It may be best if we discussed this again when—"

"She didn't, did she?"

"You must try to accept—"

"She didn't, did she?"

"James—"

"Did she?"

"No. No, she did not."

James turned the doorknob slowly, and left the room.

It made no odds to him—he didn't need her—he didn't need anyone—he didn't need anyone to help him—he could help himself—help himself to everything he needed—help himself tonight down in the study—

He was going to be a Rich Man.

He was going to be a Thief.

By tomorrow he'd be gone—he'd be somewhere safe where nobody could touch him—

Nobody was ever going to touch him—

Nobody was ever going to hurt him—hurt him—hurt him—hurt him—

He tugged out the dart and sucked the blood off his forearm.

James Edward Greville was going to be all right.

31

He waited and listened. Moonlight. Only the sound of his heart, and the slow breathing of water. Almost all the lights in the house had gone out now. He pulled the raft gently free.

He clambered aboard it. It lurched and then steadied. With the bag of provisions gripped by his knees, he started to paddle. The raft floated forward, out from the shore.

The splash of the paddle made echoes, like whispers. There were more echoes too, in his head, the whispers and laughter from last time. He tried not to hear them.

He pressed on alone.

Halfway there: the raft in the open, exposed now perhaps to eyes from the house or the garden. *No looking back, that's what I say. Best motto.* He didn't turn round.

The paddle struck bottom. He eased himself down and waded on up to the island, dragging the raft to the reed bed. The water felt cold. At the edge of the pine trees, he listened. No sound from the house or the garden to show he'd been spotted. And no sound from Ben yet. Only the ducks were awake.

He made his way round to the cabin.

He stopped when he saw it. For a long time he stood there, just looking. The food in the bag seeped through to his shirt front. Perhaps it was too wet to eat now. Not that it mattered. Ben wasn't here.

The cabin was wrecked. Numbly, James stared at the tumble of logs and tarpaulin, the remnants of cord that Ben had saved up for out of his wages. Ben couldn't have done this. Couldn't have gone.

Ben had gone. James stood a while longer. Then he moved forward. He pulled out a chair from the wreckage and wiped the seat clean with his shirtsleeve. He laid the food down on it gently. He didn't know why.

The island was empty.

He paused on the shoreline facing the beech copse. The lake was pure silver, the moon deep inside it, bright as a coin. He turned his face from it.

A yard farther on he crouched down as if puzzled. He reached out to touch what he'd found on the shingle.

Don't you touch, James. Or you'll get it all over you.

Slowly he drew back his finger. He knew what he'd touched. It was blood.

His body froze rigid.

It's all right. It's not mine, James. Not my blood.

Only his eyes moved. They followed the stain to the edge of the water. The body was flung there, like a limp wet rag.

Not Ben. James knew now.

Not mine, James. Not my blood. It's Beech's.

Not Ben who had done this.

The tiny gray skull had been smashed.

32

He waited and listened. Darkness. Only the sound of his heart, and the slow breathing from inside the bedroom. The light at the foot of the door had gone out now. He turned the knob gently and crept on in.

With his back to the door, he waited again.

Less dark here than out in the passage: the curtains were open to let in a smolder of moonlight. Hot, though. The heat was like glue, trickling down his whole body. His pajama trousers were stuck to his thighs. But it made no odds. Heat or no heat, it'd soon all be over. Upstairs in the wardrobe his bag was packed ready; beside it, T-shirt and jeans, his socks and his sneakers. A two-minute change, then out through the kitchen. Over the lawn and away down the driveway. Shot of the place, on his own for good.

Only one more thing that he needed.

His eyes inched their way round the bedroom, probing at each clump of shadow, giving it recognizable shape. The old leather chair by the window. The bath robe hooked on the door to the bathroom. The medicine bottles and books on the table. The black wooden cross on the wall by the bedstead. The bedstead itself. His eyes came to rest now. He'd got to be sure that the old bloke was sleeping: once he was sure, he could do what he'd planned on. And this time there'd be no mistakes.

He watched. The details sharpened. The bony gray bundle of sheeting, swelling and sagging in time with the breathing. The breathing loud now, filling the bedroom, but deep and steady and unsuspecting. And helpless. James's lip curled upward, tight on his teeth, in a grin. The old bloke was out cold. Dead to the world. Even colder and deader than he was in the daytime. Not scary now, only pathetic. A bundle of bones—

A movement. A catch of the breath and a stir of the sheeting. James stiffened. Waited. A clock by the bedside ticked out his heartbeats, the luminous hands at a quarter to two. Then stillness again, and the same slow rhythm. There'd been no waking. Just dreaming, maybe. Dreaming? It hardly seemed likely. Not the type to go in for anything human. Too cold and dead to dream dreams.

For a moment James tried to remember his own dreams, the ones that he knew he'd been having here, over and over. Why could he never recall them? Maybe because he just didn't want to. Maybe he knew that what he'd been dreaming had scared him, scared him too much to remember. Nightmares, not dreams. He reckoned he'd had one tonight too, before he came down here. He could still feel its echoes—

So what? He'd always had dreams. Dreams couldn't hurt him. Nothing could hurt him, not anymore. . . . *Scared to remember?* No way was he scared. He was through with all that. He was in control. He was getting the cash and getting clean out. Hitching a lift wherever a truck was willing to take him. He was going to be on his own now. Going to be all right.

He was waiting too long.

He lifted his eyes from the bundle of sheeting and fixed them on something beyond it. There—what he'd come for, by the wall, by the headboard. Another bundle, draped on a chair, with the walking-canes hooked at the ready. A scrawny black bundle. A suit of black clothes.

His lip tightened again. And somewhere deep in his stomach, another tightness, a hard shell of hatred. He felt glad of it. Safe now. Protected. No one could touch him while this was inside him. Just let *anyone* try and touch him. Just let them try.

He moved.

His feet made no sound on the carpet. The end of the bed now, and still no telltale change in the breathing. One step at a time he made his way up to the headboard. He crouched by the chair.

His hand slipped into the dark folds of clothing.

His eyes watched the head on the pillow beside him. The face was towards him, so close to his own that the breath touched his forehead.

He probed.

A faint jingle. A glint of a chain in his fingers. He followed it link by link to the waistband. Unhooked it. Lifted it upward, feeling its tension increasing. Then a sudden loud clinking from inside the pocket, the keys awaking. He froze.

Waited.

The clock like a time bomb. The racing of sweat down his body.

Waited.

On his forehead, the slow steady breath.

He lifted again. Felt the weight at the end of the chain growing heavy. The keys emerging. Dangling freely. His fist closed round them.

He crept from the room.

The study. The smells he remembered from daytime. The smells that he hated. Old books and old woodwork. More alive now, more real in the darkness. Like a presence, awake and on guard.

He closed the door softly behind him.

The room was heavy with shadows, but the window showed clearly. Showed what he wanted, waiting for him to approach it. The desk.

He moved across. In the window recess he paused, looking out. Exposed now, he thought, to eyes from the garden. What eyes? No eyes. His great-uncle sleeping. Sarah sleeping. No eyes. Only the massed shape of beeches, silent watchers. Why did trees look nearer at night?

A flutter inside him. His fear coming back.

Fear of what, for God's sake?

His old fear. Of the darkness. The nighttime. Of things waking up in the nighttime, inside his head.

He drove the feeling down fiercely.

No fear. No eyes. Only old beeches, old shadows. Only the desk. His great-uncle's desk, where he'd had to sit waiting the first day he'd come here. The scratch of the pen. The scratch of the voice that had questioned him, lectured him. Told him his mother—

The memory clenched on his stomach, tightened the hard shell of hatred inside him.

Screw him. Screw her. Screw the darkness.

None of them had any power to hurt him, to stop him from doing the job that he'd fixed on—

He made his way round to the drawer. Crouched down beside it. His hands smelt of metal. Hot keys. Six keys. Five of them big, too big for the hole that his finger could feel now. He guided the sixth one forward, along the side of his thumbnail. The three metal teeth at the tip of the shaft chattered a little, fumbling their way round the edge of the keyhole. Then sank in, and bit sharply. Turned slowly upward. His ears caught a tiny click.

He sat back on his haunches, sweat dripping from him. Then he raised himself up and took hold of the handle. He was all right now. All right. The drawer was unlocked. And no sound of waking. No sound in the room, and no movement. Nothing but shadows.

Don't look at the room. Don't look at the shadows. Only shadows, that's all. Don't look.

Just open the drawer now. Take what's inside it.

He pulled. The drawer moved a hair's breadth, then stuck.

Again. Gentle as hell, though.

Another movement. A tiny relenting.

Come on, sod you.

It came. Two inches. Sudden and violent with a loudness of wood against wood, like a scream.

He froze where he stood, his fingers locked to the handle. The echo still squealed in his ears. Squealed in the silence. He waited.

Don't let him hear. Not now. Don't let him come.

Sweat ran from his hair, stinging his eyeballs.

Don't let him come—

He blinked it away. Listened. Nothing.

The great tall tailor always comes—

One minute. Two. No sound. No door. No footstep.

Don't let him come—

Three minutes. Four. No sound.

Always comes—

Always comes—

Listened.

Won't come—not now—

Nothing.

No panic—

But somehow he knew that the fuse of his panic was lit now. His time was running out.

He forced his eyes downward. The drawer was two inches open. Just one more inch was all that he needed. Then he could slip in his hand.

Bracing one palm on the side of the desktop, he pulled. Eased again. It was coming. A widening gap. Enough now.

He edged in his hand, to the wrist.

His fingers groped forward, probed in the darkness. Then, bit by bit, he drew them back into the open. He stood there, eyes closed, not believing. He was holding the bundle of notes.

How many? A hundred? Two hundred? Two hundred fivers? Too big for fivers . . . Get out of here now—

He turned the wad round and round, feeling. And he knew there was something wrong with it somehow—

Just get the hell out—

He felt his hand reaching forward. Pressing the switch of the desk lamp. A dazzle of blindness. Then the words leaping up at him. Scrawled in pencil on top of the bundle: *For James.*

He stared at them numbly. Then watched himself lifting the thick rubber band. He read the other words, hidden beneath it. He switched off the lamp.

His numbness left him. As if the thing he was holding had just come alive in his fingers he dropped it away from him, slamming it into the drawer. He turned the key on it, backing away from it, out of the study. Opening the door of his great-uncle's bedroom, he slung the keys in on the carpet and bolted away up the staircase. He threw himself down on his bed in the darkness and curled himself up with his arms round his head.

It was over.

The dream he'd been having was breaking. If he let himself, now, he'd remember. He mustn't. Mustn't remember. He was scared.

He scrambled down farther, cocooning himself in the sheeting. He wanted someone to hold him. *It was only a dream, James. Only a dream, James. Dreams aren't real.*

But it had been real.

His dream had been real, he'd touched it, it was down there now, in that drawer in the study. It hadn't been banknotes—

He buried his face in the mattress.

It had been an old book, without covers. *Robinson Crusoe.* And words scrawled across it. *For James. From Ben.*

33

They stood together, down in the orchard. It was dark now. Ben's voice was a whisper, his face turned away.

"There's no helping it, James. Not anymore. I'm not running anymore."

"What are you going to do, then?"

"Going back, like I've been told. To the Home. Early tomorrow."

"You can't do that."

"I can't do any other."

"But you hate it there. You said you'd never go back. You said it'd be the end of you, going back there."

"I can't do any other, James."

"But you can. Father can't make you go back if you don't want to. You've got all night, Ben. He's in bed already with one of his headaches, and there's only Clara still around. If you make a run for it now—"

"Been running away half my life, seems to me. Always get you back in the end though, they do, like I said. Worse then."

"You can't let him do this to you."

"It's already done. Done this afternoon it was, when I got spotted on the island. Daft, that was. Might've got away if I'd known, swum for it like, but I didn't know, not till the boat came. Didn't even know your father had got a boat, not till then."

"He hadn't. He had it brought here specially. And he didn't even tell me. He didn't even tell me you'd been seen."

"Don't take on, James."

"He didn't even tell me he'd brought you back over. He could at least have told me that. Can't you see what he's like now?"

"There's no helping it, I told you. Two or three years maybe, and I'll be out of the Home for good. Find another post then I can, another garden. Keep me going, that will, thinking about it. Thinking about this and all, time I've been here. Best thing that ever happened to me, this was."

"Ben, listen. We can go together."

"Go where?"

"Anywhere. Away. I'll come with you. Don't say no. I can't stay here, not with him."

"Course you can. Where you belong, this is. Don't know you're born, you don't, being here."

"I can't stay."

"Got to. Can't both be leaving. Relying on you, I am."

"What?"

"Think of you, I will, carrying on where I left off. Night-time, up top-field. Spring-traps, like."

James closed his eyes.

"I hate him, Ben. I hate him so much."

"Not going to change things, hating."

"How can you say that when you know what he did? He didn't have to do that, did he? Smashing up the place you made—"

"I shouldn't have done it, maybe, not without asking. And I shouldn't have taken the stuff from the house."

"You didn't take it. I did. It was my own stuff. And the brandy wasn't stealing, it was for Beech."

"What's done's done now."

"Ben, he killed him. Can't you even hate him for that?"

"Don't make it harder for me."

"*He killed Beech.*"

"Yes. I'm that tired, James, I can't talk anymore. I'll be turning in now. Be gone come morning, before you're up, like as not. . . . Meet up again someday, I reckon. Good, that'll be."

"Ben, why? Why are you doing this? Why aren't you taking your chance? You could go now. . . . There's something else, isn't there?"

"Don't, James."

"There's something you haven't told me, isn't there? Please tell me."

For the first time, Ben turned towards him. His face was in shadow, but the tracks down his cheeks showed clearly. He didn't wipe them away.

"Yes. There's something else. I've promised, James, that's what it is. Promised your father I'll be here come morning, ready for leaving. If I'm not here waiting—"

"You can't let something like that stop you."

"—if I'm not here waiting, he's going to send Midge back, too."

James didn't move or answer. For a long moment he stared as if not believing. Then he suddenly raced away.

"James . . . James, where are you off?"

"I'm going to see him."

"You can't do that. It won't help any. Leave it be."

James ran without turning, past the stables and into the garden, on up the lawn towards the French windows. He heard Ben's footsteps coming behind.

The drawing room was in shadow. Only one of the lamps was still burning, an oil lamp on the piano. He lifted it up as Ben rushed in.

"James, don't go to him. It'll only bring more trouble."

"I'm going to see him."

"Don't do it. Please."

He felt Ben's hand on his shoulder. He shrugged it fiercely away.

Then his fingers were suddenly empty.

The oil lamp fell. Its falling splashed flames on the carpet. He watched them moving, orange and blue, across to the window and climbing the curtains. Somehow he knew that he ought to do something to stop them. But he couldn't, his legs had gone dead.

Shock. You've gone into shock. His brain gave him the message, then its messages seemed to stop coming. Only his eyes were left working. There was nothing to do but watch.

Like watching a film in slow motion, a silent film that flickered and crackled. He watched Ben's face. It looked frightened. It was turned towards him, mouth moving, making words but no noises, cheeks dancing, catching the light.

James wanted to reach out and hold him, to tell him he mustn't be frightened. But Ben had gone from him, so far away now, like part of the film. And dragging so hard at the curtains. He mustn't. He shouldn't do that, it was dangerous, his hands would start burning. James ought to warn him, they weren't curtains at all, they were fire.

Fire climbing, up to the heavy brass pole attached to the top of the window. And fire falling, the pole falling, and somebody screaming.

Was it Ben screaming?

How could he be screaming, lying face downward? With the pole like that, in the back of his head?

It's all right. It's not mine, James. Not my blood. It's Beech's.

But Ben had been lying. It *was* his own blood after all, then.

James watched the slow spreading, out of the hair to the collar, and on down the sleeve to the ruin of fingers.

How much more magic have you got up your sleeve, Ben?

How much more blood?

Maybe this was just more of the magic. Fire magic. Blood magic. Blood to put out the fire.

So why was Ben screaming?

Ben wasn't screaming.

Poor Ben.

James turned and ran. And the screaming and fire ran with him, but Ben didn't follow. Down through the garden, knowing the screams were his own, and his own legs burning. There were faces, his father's and Clara's, but they flickered and faded away as he passed them. Another face now, and arms that were reaching to hold him.

"Help me. Please help me."

"I'm here, James."

And Midge was with him, pale in the darkness, her arms around him.

"It's all right, James."

"He's dead. He's gone now. . . ."

"Gone now, James. Over now. I'm here." And he knew that it wasn't Midge anymore. It was Sarah.

"It's gone now, James. It's over now."

"He's dead."

"You've been dreaming. Walking a bit in your sleep, that's all, out here in the garden."

"There was blood. It was my fault. I killed him."

"Only a dream, James."

"The blackbird. He's dead."

"Hush now. It's all right now."

"It was the blackbird, outside my window. He sang to me. And I killed him."

"Hush." She pressed him to her.

"Buried now. Under the rubble."

"Don't cry now. It's over."

"Help me."

"All over. It's gone away. The dream won't come back anymore. I know, James. I know these things. It won't come back to you, ever again."

"How do you know?"

"Because I'm here now. And you've come to me, and asked me to help."

He clung to her, rocking, a child again, and listened to the gentle sleep of her voice.

"And because I've seen the same unhappiness before, maybe. In someone else like you who's needed help but never come to ask it. Someone I've loved like I've loved you, from the beginning, even though he never knew."

He looked up at her and her face swam in the darkness and seemed young again. So close to him, but gazing far beyond him, away across the lawn.

"Someone with worse dreams than yours, James. Dreams that have walked in his mind, always. And I've stayed with him, because he needed me."

"It was him, then. My great-uncle."

"It was always him, and never any other. Your great-uncle. Your poor Uncle James."

"Yes."

And gently, closing his eyes, he felt the arm of Midge round his shoulders, and he let her take him, back to the house.

34

As I sit here in the study, at this desk at which my father once sat,
I am older than he was when he died.

If I look at the empty chair on the opposite side of the desk, I can
see myself sitting there as the boy I once was. And I can hear my
father's voice speaking across the desk-top from the chair in which I
sit now.

And it is all so clear.

Why have my dreams been so clear in the past six days?

Since the boy first came to this house.

James Greville turned his face to the window. He looked
out. On the bench down by the copse Sarah was shelling
peas in the lap of her apron. She seemed cheerful today. She
must have slept well, then, in spite of the heat which had
tumbled his own sleep with nightmares. But the weather
had now at last lifted. The morning was blue, with a breeze
high in the beeches. Soon, perhaps, the boy would have
finished his breakfast, would appear on the terrace.

The boy. My great-nephew.

James.

They were wrong about you, James. I saw that on the first day
you came here. For all your stealing, you are no thief.

There is no greed in your eyes.

You would not have succeeded in hiding it from me. It would
have shown as you looked around you, at all that I possess.

At all that you will possess.

Has it occurred to you, even once, that one day all this—all these
acres, the lake, the Lodge—are going to be yours?

No, you are no thief.

The terrace was crisp with sunlight. Should he take a short walk there, as Sarah had suggested at breakfast? If he beckoned, she would leave her bench and come to him, to support him.

He drew his eyes from her, back to the room.

It was something else that I saw in your eyes, not greed.

And that is why I have dreamt so much since you came to this house, James.

You have opened old wounds.

Not the wounds in my legs, the fire-wounds where the skin has tightened. It is other wounds which you have opened, the ones I have tried to keep hidden.

Do you know how you did that, James, on that first day we met, in this study?

You reminded me, you see, of someone I have tried to forget.

He looked across at the empty chair where the boy had sat waiting, withdrawn and afraid. That was when the wounds had opened, the memories awoken. The boy had reminded him so clearly. Not of Ben. Of himself.

Of myself as I became, James, after it all happened. And of myself as I am now. Withdrawn. Afraid.

Afraid of what?

Of affection? Of rejection, perhaps.

Of being hurt again.

That is why I have become like my father.

He raised his eyes. James had appeared on the terrace. He stood at its edge for a moment, outside the window, looking across at the beech copse. Then he made his way down to the lawn.

Over the years, I have watched myself turn into my own father. I have heard myself speaking to you with my father's voice.

It is safer that way.

But you know that yourself. You have learned the same lesson already. That is what I saw in your eyes, when we met here.

Do you know something else, James?

Over the years, you will watch yourself turn into me.

James moved across the lawn. When he came near the bench he faltered, uncertain. Sarah glanced up and spoke for an instant. Then he went on past her, into the copse.

That is why your coming here was a mistake, James, perhaps; why the experiment may be a failure.

Because we are both the same, you and I.

We dare not take chances.

In the shadows behind her, James stopped and looked back towards her.

We are both afraid.

35

James stood at the edge of the beeches. His eyes took aim. Wrist cocked, fingers tensed, he paused as if to will himself to do it.

His hand moved.

The steel spike flashed upward, a long sharp arc against the sunlight. Then it plummeted and vanished.

He watched the ring of ripples fade away across the lake.

"Did you . . ."

He hesitated, shifting himself on the bench-arm and turning the empty pea-pod slowly around in his fingers.

"Did you tell him? I mean—about last night?"

He didn't look at Sarah. But from the corner of his eye he saw her hands falter for a moment in their shelling of the peas.

"No, James. I didn't. Last night's forgotten. And it would trouble him maybe, being told. Because . . . James, I know how hard it is for you, believing it, but he was hoping so much that you'd be happy here."

"Is . . . is he happy here?"

"He belongs here, that's how it is, and never known any other. And he was happy once."

He looked at her now. She was smiling a little, gazing absently down at the gravel. He traced the line of her face with his eyes, wondering if it was Midge he was seeing or

Sarah. And he knew it was both, the one explaining the other. And knowing it made it easier, somehow, to sit here and talk.

"But there've been things in his life that have changed him, that's all, James, and made him like he seems now. Not always like they seem though, people aren't. And always reasons for what they become. That's what we have to try and understand a bit, maybe. . . . I've been with him so long."

She sat silent, as if no longer aware of his presence. And he knew that her eyes were seeing things that were far away in the past now. Half a century away, he thought, like my dreams. My great-uncle's dreams. The dreams that we've shared.

How had it happened? He didn't know. Were they so like each other? Is that what it was? Perhaps.

I don't know. But it's happened. I've seen the past through my dreams. I've seen his past, through his dreams. And, somehow, I'm glad.

He listened.

"I remember the first time I saw him. Down in the orchard, that was, and him so young and shy. 'Master James' he was to me then, but never a one for wanting to show he was above you, not like his father. A terrible man, his father was. But there, perhaps his father had his own reasons, too, for being like he was, and his own sadness, and us with no way of knowing."

"What was his mother like?"

"Oh, quite the lady, Mrs. Greville. But we saw less of her. Kept herself to herself, like, and not much time for Master James she hadn't. More taken up with young Edward— your grandfather, that would've been, but only a baby that first year I came here. Always a poor sickly thing, Master

Edward, and away down to the coast with his mother most summers, to help with his chest.

"Yes, it must've been a lonely old time for your great-uncle and no mistake, and him with his bad dreams when he was little. Used to wake up crying fit to burst, old Clara used to say—the cook here at the Lodge, Clara was in those days, and always the one to go to him to comfort him, never his mother or father. A book he used to have, poems or some such, she said, that upset him. Nasty thing it was by all accounts, and him so on his own and full of fancies."

"Is it . . . is it still here?"

"Oh, no. Gone many a year now. Your grandfather Edward took it with him, as I recall, when he went off to London. Though what became of it after, I don't know. Still down there somewhere it'll be, if it hasn't been destroyed in the meantime."

"Yes."

"Yes, a real mother to him old Clara was. Understood need, did Clara, without asking. But she died not long after, when he needed her most."

"After? After what?"

Why had he asked her? he wondered. Why did he so much need her to share with him something he already knew?

She brought her eyes back to her lap and picked up a pea-pod. But she left it unopened.

"It's . . . it's what you were asking about, James, that morning in the kitchen. About the bit of the house that's gone now."

He waited.

"There was a fire, James, that first summer I came here. That bit of the house got burned down."

"Why didn't you tell me that morning?"

"Oh, I don't know. It's just that your great-uncle doesn't like it recalled, and . . . well, perhaps I didn't think you'd . . ."

She turned her face round towards him. He looked away.

"James, maybe it's wrong of me talking of these things with him not knowing. But—but maybe it's wrong of him, too, keeping them hidden and people not understanding him better, the way he's become. . . . The fire, James. It was him that caused it. Your great-uncle. Accidental it was, but it changed him. He's never been back to that bit of the garden, won't have it touched even now. And so long ago. Forgive and forget, that's what it should be. But he can't forgive himself, and he can't forget. The fire's still with him, James, and still burning. It's in his dreams, always. And other things too, things I can't talk of. But maybe it's enough, what I've talked of already, to help you try and understand. . . . Well, there, I've said it now as shouldn't have. But it needed saying, for all that."

"Thanks."

Would she feel the need to say something else, too?

James, you wouldn't ever tell on me, would you?

He waited again. But she was silent, calmly shelling the peas.

"Have you got any plans for this morning, James?"

"Not really. I'll be fine, though. I'll just walk a bit, perhaps, round the grounds."

"It's a nice old place for walking, this weather."

"Yes."

"And off to see Mr. Dawes tomorrow, so we must get some bus times sorted out. It seems to have come round so fast somehow, this first week. I—I hope it'll go all right. You a bit nervous?"

"No."

"I'm glad . . . James, you—you don't have to go telling

him about yesterday morning if you don't want. Nothing'll come of it, Joyce said. Past's past, and it was only a silly mistake—"

"I know."

"Well, there then." She gathered the empty pea-pods together and sat back for a moment, looking up at the sun in the branches. "Seems a shame to go in, really. I'm going to try and winkle your great-uncle out of his study in a bit, for a walk on the terrace. Do his poor legs good." She smiled. "Not but that I'll probably get a real old kick in the teeth for my trouble."

"Sorry?"

"Head bitten off. Used to it by now though, I am. And he never means it, not really. But it'll take more than old Midge to change his ways now, maybe, and get through that shell of his to what's underneath." She turned to James, smiling again. "That's what he used to call me, that first summer. Midge. Not now, though. Not since the fire. My proper name—Sarah—it's been ever after. Funny—I always liked Midge better somehow. My brother's name for me, that was."

"You—you didn't ever say you had a brother."

"Oh, yes. Yes, I had a brother. Used to work in the grounds here in the old days. You'd have liked him, James."

"Would I?"

"He loved this place so much. Knew every inch of it. And nobody could help knowing it and loving it the same way, just being with him. Yes, he had the sunlight in him all right, Ben did, and ready to give it to others. But there, he was taken from us early. And all that was a long time ago."

She eased herself to her feet.

"Well, I'll be getting along. All this talking about the past, and me with today to see to, not yesterday. No looking back, that's what I say. Best motto."

"Yes."

He watched her go from him, back to the house.

James walked through the grounds. His path brought him back to the margin of the beech copse. He paused there for an instant, opposite the house.

He tipped back his head and stared straight above him at the dazzle. The treetops were all blazing. There was fire in the leaves and in the branches. Ben was burned now. Ben was gone.

But James was here. And one more kick in the teeth wouldn't hurt him. He was used to it by now.

He moved across the lawn towards the study. In a moment he'd be in there.

There was fire on the window. He couldn't see if the face was turned towards him or turned from him. But it didn't really matter. The fire was only sunlight, after all.